Plague and Rage

Plague and Rage

The Black Death and the Peasants' Revolt of 1381

PAUL BANNISTER

LUME BOOKS

LUME BOOKS

Published in 2022 by Lume Books

Copyright © Paul Bannister 2022

The right of Paul Bannister to be identified as the author of this work
has been asserted by them in accordance with the Copyright, Design
and Patents Act, 1988.

ISBN 978-1-83901-517-5

Typeset using Atomik ePublisher from Easypress Technologies

www.lumebooks.co.uk

Introduction

Inside a lattice-walled, yellow-felted yurt on a windswept steppe, a Tatar horseman slept the sleep of the weary.

His name Erdene meant 'jewel' and he was a khan of the *Altan Ordu:* the Golden Horde of Uzbeg Khan's nomadic Mongols, Turks and Tatars that had sacked a Polish royal city in the previous year, 1341. Erdene the Tatar was an empire builder, a conqueror whose army devastated vast regions, but his own doom arrived in undramatic form, in the shape of a small brown insect: a flea. It hopped onto his exposed inner wrist in search of a meal of human blood, landed unnoticed as the man slept, and pierced his skin with its small fangs.

The flea's mouth, designed to pierce, pump numbing saliva into the wound and quietly suck up its victim's blood, worked as it should, and the insect shared with Erdene the Tatar a deadly legacy it had itself received from a brown rat in a caravanserai on the Silk Road a matter of days before.

The legacy was a bacterium called *Yersinia pestis* that causes bubonic plague. The disease that had raged across Europe in the time of the Roman emperor Justinian had lain quiet for six centuries while the Mongols swept across the land with death, fire and rapine. But now the plague was stirring again in the Celestial Mountains of Turkistan and the ruthless conquerors of China were in no manner as lethal as the invisible bacterium carried by a single tiny flea. In its newest iteration, the Black Death would halve the population of the European continent, bringing death to tens of millions of people.

The Tatar Erdene died horribly and painfully within two days of that fleabite, coughing blood, his innards collapsing in bloody flux. His body rotted in a putrefying mass of black boils, as big as apples, that swelled in his crotch and armpits; his breath was a miasma like foul marsh gas. Those who tended him died too, infected by the very air he exhaled. They and he were among the first of the Great Pestilence's new victims. The death of the Tatar and of the millions like him lost to plague would reshape civilisation, and it all began with a single fleabite. Yet, in the very place where plague and death began, a once-enslaved boy would show the way to freedom for tens of thousands of Englishmen.

Chapter 1

Quarterstaff

Everyday matters filled my mind as I trudged home at workday's end. The chores of a rural peasant never end. Those beeches down by the rill need pollarding, I thought resignedly, and the hornbeams could use some lopping as well. Also, I'll have to release the pig into the woods to pasture her on beechmast and acorns. I have no idea why the verderers are so stubborn at denying us peasants the old privilege, because eating acorns can kill the forest ponies, and pigs rooting about not only remove that potential poison, they also turn the soil, breaking up compaction; they even fertilise the ground. Despite all those positives, letting your beasts forage is forbidden except for a couple of months a year and the punishment if you are caught can be savage.

I decided I'd risk it. I'd let the sow out after dark and bring her in before dawn. The local verderer was a lazy man and I knew from my stealthy excursions to poach rabbits or pheasants he would not be up and about that early. Anyway, the pig was carrying a litter and she could use some extra nourishment from pannage. It's a poor thing when you can't even let an animal have the feed God has provided. Right now, I'm hungry, but a big man can't look forward to his supper with much enthusiasm when it's just a soupy pottage of dried beans, peas and onions. That is not enough to fuel you after a long day marling, boosting the acidic Kentish soil with clay, lime and compost. It's hard work digging in the straw and manure we'd so carefully saved but it's the only way to get tilth good enough to grow your crops. I grinned to myself at the internal conversation. 'Tom Thatcher,' I chided myself, 'just get on with it. You must grow enough for Lizzie and any baby she gets, as well as for yourself. Your task is to improve that soil.'

All I knew was that we in the village farmed several hundred strips of land divided up from three large unfenced fields, a third of them left fallow. The strips, called selions, are cultivated by families of villeins – peasants like me who are tied to the land – and we work it from Prime to Nones, or nine long hours a day as the clergy count time. Some strips yield good crops but other serfs seemed to have only poor soils in their allotments that allowed their unlucky families a skimpy subsistence of crops. I was lucky. My selions ran downhill and drained well, so gave a fair yield of barley, oats and vegetables like carrots, cabbages and onions.

In a common area of bottom land, we peasants share the work and grow grain for bread, pottage and ale. Harvesting it is back-breaking work and timing is everything. After it's cut – cruel, stooping work with hand sickles – the grain is left to dry and is turned with pitchforks for a time. If there's a downpour during those days, the crop can be ruined, and it will be a near-starvation year for the whole village. From our share in a good harvest, we get five or so loaves of bread per week, some of them rye, the others wheat. Perhaps Lizzie and I do better than other peasants because I sometimes slip into the fallow field where we pasture our animals and collect their dung to spread on the strip of land that gives us vegetables.

I was almost home when, doglike, I was distracted as my nostrils caught a scent of supper on the breeze. Here was our elm-framed cottage and I cast a critical eye at the thatch whose top layer of straw I'd replaced a few months earlier. It is good for a tradesman to show off his work and I refresh my thatch every few years, long before it needs the work. Not that I had much thatching trade, except for reluctantly doing that unpaid labour for my manorial lord.

Almost at the threshold now, I called a greeting and my woman Elizabeth showed her face at the door and smiled at me. I set aside my iron-tipped, wooden spade, caught Lizzie around the waist and kissed her. She pushed me away. 'Tom, you stink!' she mock-protested.

'Aye,' I agreed. 'You dig in Henrietta's muck and sty straw all day and you'd be a bit smelly, too. I'll wash before supper.' Such as it is, I thought sourly, remembering the time a month before when our local lord had called me to the hall where they were feasting Prior Hamo of Rochester Cathedral.

Baron Roger of Bowerfield manor had heard of my skill with a quarterstaff and sent for me, one of his villeins, to demonstrate using the fighting stick. It would be an after-dinner entertainment for his churchman guest. My opponent was one of the baron's household, a burly soldier called Simon Ottercombe and I had eyed him cautiously when we met outside the hall. We nodded, unspeaking, and began assessing each other. He was tall, two clothyards height, and we looked level at each other, eye to eye, for I am a big man even though I have not quite attained a score of years. I noted that his nose had been broken and badly reset, which implied he wasn't invincible. He wore a broad leather band on his left wrist, and I caught a gleam from it which told me he had a concealed weapon, probably a punching knife, hidden there.

On his feet were heavy nailed boots, an advantage for me as they would slow his footwork. A steward approached as we surveyed each other. 'Tom?' he asked.

I nodded. 'Aye.'

'Would you like a trencher of stew?'

My stomach urged me to accept but I shook my head. 'I'm fine, sir,' I said. I didn't want to be sluggish around this Ottercombe fellow.

'You, Simon?' the steward asked.

He nodded. 'Be good, that would.'

'Wait here, I'll bring you something. Small beer?' Ottercombe indicated pleasure with a grunt. This time the steward merely raised an eyebrow at me and I shook my head.

We sat on a bench outside the hall, me sniffing odours of roasting meat from the spits inside the hall, Ottercombe snuffling like a pig at trough as he gulped down his stew, then ate the entire trencher, a hollowed-out loaf that had held it. He swilled down a quart of beer, belched loudly and sprawled back, content and confident, awaiting our bout. I looked around, trying to decipher the lettering on a wall hanging, for I can both read and write, thanks to my childhood days with the monks who wanted to train me as a cleric. I ended that without regrets when my father died and my mother needed extra help on our land. Now, no friar, I am a full-fledged farmer and tradesman; although this night I was to be a fighter.

Soon enough, a man-at-arms approached carrying two hawthorn staves of equal size, about seven feet long. I chose one, Ottercombe took the other and we were led into the candle-bright hall where servants were clearing platters away from the trestle tables. I looked around – I was admitted only rarely to the hall – and probably gaped at the colourful hangings behind the top table where Baron Roger and Prior Hamo lounged on a dais above the trestle tables. We passed a large open fire set up on raised flagstones in the hall's centre where boys turned several spits as they roasted what looked like the body of a stag, a whole wild boar and several dozens of chickens, hares and waterfowl. A troop of perspiring red-faced cooks collected the meat drippings to baste the roasts; a scurry of bakers hurried past with trays of pies made in a huff paste of flour, suet and hot water. That coffyn – a casing of stiff pasty – was nearly inedible, but the peasants who gathered outside the hall would be grateful of it, soaked as it was in tasty juices. It was a rare benefit for them to taste meat: something that came only at feast days.

Everywhere a swarm of pages bustled between buffets and tables to select, carve and deliver to their masters choice cuts of meats from the stepped buffet shelves. Those gentry ate delicately with their fingers but on the lower tables, where the pages delivered whole, smoking joints of meat, lesser mortals hacked off lumps which they ate from the point of a knife.

In front of the top tables, servants had taken away some trestle tables to clear a space for our combat. The steward hushed the minstrels and made a brief announcement of our contest saying that the bout would end when blood was drawn on a fighter's head. The grandees gestured for servants to bring towels, ewers and bowls of scented water to wash their fingers as they finished the meat courses and settled back to watch our combat before commencing on the pastries, cheeses and fruits they knew would come next.

Ottercombe and I stepped apart and faced each other; the steward called 'Commence!' and we moved forward. I shuffled with my right foot, keeping my left a pace back as support. My stance was a little wider than my shoulders. I held the base of my staff in my left hand and placed my right about a quarter distance up the shaft. It's why it's called a quarterstaff.

Ottercombe was circling. I stepped to his inside, dropped my staff to the horizontal and slid my right hand down. The staff's length makes it superior to a sword for you can fight at greater distance. My opponent feinted left, swung right and kicked me painfully on the kneecap as he swung his staff. I blocked the swing and, all in the same movement, stabbed my blackthorn into his unguarded midsection. He doubled over gasping and I sent an overhead blow that cracked him above the temple and removed a neat square of skin. The fight was over as he went to his knees and the blood poured out of his head.

Half the hall cheered, half booed and stamped their feet at the brevity of the 'demonstration'. The baron looked rueful; the prior yawned as he digested the venison he'd eaten. Baron Roger beckoned me forward. I stepped over Ottercombe's doubled-up body where he wheezed on the floor and was handed a silver long cross penny. 'Very fast, er, Tom,' said the baron. 'I'll have to find you a better opponent for your next display.' I knuckled my forehead and with that I was dismissed.

Chapter 2

Strictures

Weeks later, at our own frugal supper, I still held close the memory of that crowded, fire-and-candlelit hall with its patterned tiles, plastered and painted walls; of the noisy, feasting yeomen; of luxurious white bread in wicker baskets; of the array of puddings and pies displayed on stepped buffets along one wall and of the glorious smells of roasting meats that permeated the whole hall.

In our hovel, chewing tasteless, dark rye bread and mopping up my pottage of beans and onions, I sighed in discontent. 'Lizzie,' I addressed my wife, 'why do they get all the good things?' I nodded in the direction of the manor. 'I work hard and I work three days a week for them without pay. They say it's rent for this' – I waved my knife in the direction of our allotted strips of ploughland – 'but they always want something more.'

Lizzie said softly: 'It isn't so bad, Tom. We have our house…' but I interrupted.

'Liz, we're bonded. We're almost slaves. We can't even leave this place without Baron Roger's permission. We're villeins: we can't own a bit of land even if we could afford it. We have to pay taxes to the king; we pay tithes to the church; our whole family except the wife must work extra 'boon' days for the lord when called upon. We are commanded to take him a salmon at the quarter day of Michaelmas, a dozen hens at Christmas and twelve dozen eggs and six dozen eels at Easter. That's ironic, eh? Eels hold the souls of sinful monks and priests condemned by Saint Dunstan to do eternal penance for their sins in that slithery form, yet the monks eat their former brothers. That's how unscrupulous and self-indulgent they are.

'They work us like animals. We do extra days ploughing for no pay; we work the harvest unpaid, and our reward for all the days we spend scything is miserly: we're allowed to carry off as much cut grass as will not break the scythe handle. We are even obliged to take the baron's crops to market – again for no reward – and we must provide the cart and a beast to pull it.

'If we sell a cow or a horse, we must give the lord some of the price; if we marry off a daughter, he claims the merchet tax. You pay a fine for having a child out of wedlock and pay another tax to avoid being beaten or whipped. The lords will even find wives for their tenants but specify that any children belong to him. What kind of world makes you buy your own children?

'We can't use our own grindstone to crush grain because the abbot has a monopoly and charges us to use his. The monks at Rochester have paved the abbey with confiscated hand millstones taken from people like us. They're rubbing it in every time we attend church there and walk on someone's carved stone that's been cemented into the cloister floor. They want to remind us to take our grain to be ground at the abbey's mills for fat fees. The baron and the prior are hand in glove and spell it all out in their custumals.'

Liz laid a gentle hand on my arm. 'I've never heard that word,' she said.

'A preacher told us about it in the tavern once,' I said. 'It's a book of lists the baron keeps, like an account book of rents and services we are obliged to deliver as his villeins. It details what specific tasks certain peasants must perform. For instance, Michael, the oxherd, told me the baron's steward read him the list of his duties, as recorded in the baron's book. He must take the beasts to and from pastures each day, hobble them each night, feed them with hay and straw he must gather. He's obliged to train them to pull ploughs evenly and to tread corn and straw and, in the winter, to take the lord's cattle into the byre and feed and water them properly from Christmas Eve to Ascension Day. There's more but I can't remember it all.'

The lords' books tell us also what we cannot do. Under ancient laws we must not hunt in the forest or fish in the lakes or rivers; we must fight and plough for our various lords. If we locals want to have a market in our town, we must pay fees in solid silver coin, straight to the king. They said that old King John, brother of Lionheart, issued nearly eighty market charters and took hefty payments for each.

Even the sheriffs and their clerks – who probably paid handsome bribes to get their posts – levy extortionate dues on beer and demand taxes on things like bread, eggs, honey and hunting dogs. Townsmen pay rents, stallage tolls for markets and lastage taxes to store their goods. They pay murage to maintain the town walls, pavage to keep the streets in repair and pontage to cross a bridge. If you are a yeoman lucky enough to own land, you cannot sell it at will – there are always leases, fees, dues and levies. There's burgage for house rent, and tallage to the king for using his land. We cannot even wear the clothes we choose: sumptuary laws decree specific clothing that advertises your standing; Jews must wear a yellow conical hat, badge or ring. Even heretics and people suffering specific diseases are regulated: lepers must wear a red cap and a grey cloak and ring a bell to warn others of their approach.

Prostitutes are ordered to wear a striped hood and no finery, to distinguish them from decent women, and harlots working in the brothels of Southwark, which are mostly owned by the Bishop of Winchester, are not allowed to wear aprons. I once asked a packman about that and he laughed. 'The bishop's ecclesiastical costume includes an apron,' he chuckled, 'and I suppose he doesn't like the idea of being a frocked churchman in a hoyden's clothes.' We laughed together and he went on to tell me that the strumpets in the bishop's brothels are known as 'Winchester Geese'. 'If you're "pecked" by such a goose and get "goose bumps," heaven help you,' he said. 'You've caught the clap: the Black Lion.'

They regulate more than just one or two groups, though. Merchants and esquires are barred from wearing clothing costing more than five marks because the old king Edward wanted all to know their place; he passed laws governing the fabric, quality, colour and type of clothing suitable for each person. He decreed that extravagant apparel would not be permitted, including adornments like furs and jewels, except for those above a certain rank. He even laid down ordinances defining the number and quality of courses that may be consumed at the dining table and decreed savage punishments for traders who cheated. A baker accused of selling bread with stones in it to increase its weight would be dragged on a hurdle to a pillory, pinioned while his bread was burned under his nose, pelted by the crowds with the stones he'd used and, as a gift, pelted, too, with any dung or offal they picked up on the street.

Although some of the extensive royal timberlands – kept clear for the king's hunting pleasures – had been cleared for pastures and tillable soil, the laws and Edward were not popular. The king invited, some say even tempted, foreign workers, Flemings and Zeelanders, to Norfolk to employ their skills in the wool trade that is so lucrative for the crown. Privately, I thought Edward must have known how the locals would resent them: they were skilled and produced better wool cloth than anything to come off an English weaver's loom, so there would be jealousy. There would always be hatred for foreigners who dressed differently, who had enjoyed lives elsewhere, beyond the locals' own windswept fens, who spoke in a different tongue as if English was not good enough.

Edward knew it: he even allotted soldiers to guard the incomers' villages. And the guards were needed. The incomers were most bitterly resented by every starving, unemployed labourer who blamed his lack of work on the immigrants. They used the cheap labour of women and children to unfairly undercut honest English artisans. The villagers grumble that the incomers don't even speak proper English to us, but we have to tolerate these pampered strangers in our midst.

In another hugely unpopular bout of control, the king set wages low to please his nobles, and empowered his mayors and aldermen to impose fines on any who refused to work for those rates. With the backing of wealthy merchants, the city fathers ruled that the guilds were illegal and imprisoned the few men who tried to organise their fellows. Next, they created laws regulating both drinking and gambling, although the nobility was largely excluded and only the common people were so burdened. Worse, money was in short supply and many blamed those rich and privileged merchants who bled the wealth out of the country by buying useless luxuries like sugar, spices, porcelain and silk and sending our English gold abroad.

When we men of Bowerfield meet at the tavern or at the archery butts where the law says we must practise with the longbow every Sunday because the king needs a reserve of trained archers for his foreign wars, we mutter sourly about the crippling taxes and levies we face and complain about the half-week of free labour we are forced to perform under the feudal law of corvée. This mandates that we must work unpaid for our manorial lords.

The talk in the tavern after one particular archery practice had a comrades-in-distress tone until one man made the divisive point that, although we land-holding villeins kept our strips of soil by working for our rents, landless men like himself who often have skills as a mason, carpenter, sawyer or so forth must compete for work against others like him, so the lord of the manor can buy his services at the lowest possible rate.

A fat red-faced man shouted that he was a mason and he often had to work as a cotter or common labourer because he held no land and his usual reward was mere penny-ale, not bacon; dried-out vegetables, not fresh and only scraps of fish or meat because that was all he could afford. 'As a mason I get five pence a day. As a labourer they pay me less than two pence.'

'Ah, but!' called out a red-haired villein. 'You can travel and find better work. We cannot. We are tied to our tillage for a miserable four pence an acre per year. Try and live on that!'

Red Face shouted back: 'Aye, but you get free the food you grow and it's good. I have to buy my food!' The atmosphere was getting heated and neighbours were arguing with neighbours about who suffered the worse wrongs.

Finally, a fellow with the accents of the north country stood up and rapped his wooden beer mazer on the table for silence. 'You have to join together,' he said quietly. 'Complaining among yourselves will achieve nothing. If everyone refuses to work, the lords will have to improve matters for you.'

Alan Hardwick, who worked the strip of land next to mine, spoke up. 'What bothers me most is the way those fat monks demand what our hard work fetches,' he shouted. 'You, Tom, I know you hate them, too.'

A young fellow I knew by sight – he was from Ashlea, the next village to ours, stood up boldly. 'Those greedy friars,' he said angrily. 'They killed my baby sister.'

The room went quiet until the north countryman spoke again. 'Tell us about that, son, tell us your name.'

'I'm Walter, call me Wat. It's true: they caused our baby to die. The rain ruined our crop two years ago and we were starving hungry but they came demanding their tithe anyway. My dad gave them what we had, a few pennies, and they took our three chickens as well.' The youth stood there, embarrassed but defiant. Then he blurted: 'My mother said she didn't have milk and the baby died.'

'That's a terrible shame, son,' said the north countryman. 'Did nobody help?'

'Our curate didn't charge us to bury her and he did find some work for my dad. He makes tiles for roofs. We survived a year that way until we got a crop. Curate John was kind, not like the friars. My dad says we have to knock them off their perches.'

The red-faced man shouted, 'Amen to that!' and a grumble of agreement went around the room.

A local coppersmith named Edmund called out: 'They're too fat to get onto perches; they're eating their way into heaven! The Pope should put them all on bread and water for a while!' A roar of approval went around the room and, as the cider went down, the temperature and the arguments were increasing.

I jested loudly: 'I'll bring it up with the Pope when I see him next.' It was an old joke but it got a few grins because I had a small fame in the village as the only one there, now my father was dead, who'd actually seen the Pope.

It had been when I was a nipper of eight or so and the Pope came to Kent on his way to summon King Edward. My father and I walked the Portway to Rochester to view God's vicar on Earth in all his splendour, although we were somewhat in error about that. I heard much later that the emissary – who I also found was not the Pope – had come to order our king to Paris to bend the knee to Philip of France, who professed to be Edward's overlord. Edward held some territory in France and later even claimed the throne of France as his right, but the French argued that our monarch was a mere vassal of the French king. Or so the Pope said.

King Edward refused to go and pay homage and that was another cause of all the expensive warring between England and the Frenchies across the Channel. So, someone came to see Edward and we stood in a gaping crowd on the fine ragstone bridge in Rochester that some pious mercer had built to thank God for the fortune he'd made off our peasant labours. And we watched the high churchmen parade past in their silks and jewels when they escorted their master to meet our king. I asked my father what did a Pope do? He told me: 'He's God's man on Earth and he gives pardons out to sinners – if they can pay.' He turned away and I wondered why he grimaced, but I always remembered.

At least my jest cooled matters in the tavern and someone persisted in it. 'So, you will ask his High Holiness, will you, Tom?'

I said I'd mention it the next time we feasted together; I got a few more grins and the talk turned away from grumbling about our lot in life. I also had a quiet word with young Wat the tile maker and asked him about the good curate. 'He was at St Peter's church, Curate Raw I think, but he's not there now.'

I remembered the name; it might be useful one day, and that was where it stood for months, complaints without action although the resentments were building.

Chapter 3

Guilds

Then came the day an itinerant hedge-preacher walked into our village, set down his pack, positioned himself by the stocks and whipping post, and began to speak. In a short time, the villagers began drifting in to hear what this ragged traveller had to say and when I walked through, on my way to the smithy for some nails to repair Henrietta's sty, about fifteen locals were listening.

'You are being oppressed by your masters,' he bellowed. 'You know there are three estates: one to fight, one to pray and one to work. The nobles are the knights who enjoy fighting; the churchmen live very well for just saying prayers and the third, the peasantry, do all the work to feed and enrich the knights and priests. All men are children of God but your standing is much, much inferior to your masters' and not because of God's word. Corrupt mankind has stolen away the lives enjoyed by Adam and Eve and you deserve better.'

Someone in the small crowd shouted: 'Aye, and how do we do that without getting a flogging?'

When the growl of agreement died down, the preacher pointed dramatically westwards. 'In London, men are forming conventicles and guilds – brotherly groups to share alike and to resist the unreasonable demands of their masters. They have power over their lords when they stick together and it's a way to put money in their purses, too. These banded brothers can claim a share in purchases made by any other of them. All share the real price without just one making a profit from his brothers.

'When they are sick, their guild brothers bring them bread and wine; when they die, they sing Masses for their souls. They hold festivals on the day of their guild's patron saint; they obey agreed rules and pay fines if they break those rules. They are organised against the rich who would monopolise trade and they set standards for the craft they share so the public will trust them.' The ragged man with the silver tongue paused, then said quietly: 'We have to copy their example, gather in strength with weapons and put restraints on those who call themselves our masters! They won't be so masterful when they face a force of us. That's when they'll find that one man cannot control a crowd and, if we must, we will use violence.' We cheered him enough to frighten the chickens, for we had all suffered in some way at the hands of those who lived off our toil.

Few people paid attention to the leech gatherer, a familiar figure in Baron Roger's Kentish manor. He was normally seen barelegged, wading in watery ditches or in the shallows of ponds and lakes stirring up submerged vegetation to attract his slimy prey. Passing peasants would sometimes stop to watch in horrified fascination as he dabbed a taste of salt on the backs of the predator worms to detach them painlessly from his flesh and they would invariably ask: 'Does that hurt?'

The leech gatherer, whose name was Owen Blackburn, would wipe away the inevitable trickles of blood and say with a gap-toothed smile, 'Why no, my dear, 'tis nothing, but if I peel them off by force, their jaws may remain in my flesh and suppurate.'

'Why do you collect them?' the curious would ask. Blackburn would explain patiently, 'They remove the humours of yellow bile, blood, black bile and phlegm that can change your health.'

Sometimes, the onlooker would ask to examine the segmented brown-green worm that was almost the length of a man's smallest finger, always wanting to see the tiny teeth in its round mouth, but few were brave enough to touch the bloodsucker. Blackburn would patiently hold the worm up for inspection, mention how it could ingest five times its own weight in blood and say, 'No, its bite didn't hurt; they injected some sort of painkiller so you didn't know one had latched onto you.' Most people guessed that Blackburn's activity brought him a small income from physicians and the like who used the bloodworms on their patients to 'suck the ailment out', reduce swellings or help heal wounds and that was usually the next question.

Blackburn would smile and tell the truth when he admitted he didn't get a king's fortune for a worm. In fact, a dozen leeches would bring him a modest penny from one of his clients but he enjoyed the outdoors, he had no master and, in the depths of winter when wading in icy water was not a congenial thing, he would become an itinerant furrier. This had him tramping from village to village to sell the pelts of hares, rabbits, squirrels and even the occasional fox to wealthier folk who trimmed their clothes with fur. The meat of his catches was a bonus, as were the lampreys, fish and eels he poached to add variety to his diet.

But for all of his familiarity to the locals, Blackburn had a secret which he shared in the security of the tavern. The leech gatherer had met and been convinced by a firebrand cleric several months before, quietly to spread the word of discontent, inciting serfs and villeins to unite and demand better conditions of work and reward. The cleric, a former chaplain called John Wrawe had been outlining to any who would listen how their masters scorned and used them. The name 'Wrawe' caused ears to prick up. Some of the group remembered the young fellow who told how his baby sister had starved, weakened and died because the church took the family's small wealth as tithes. That youth had described a kindly curate called 'Raw' who buried the baby for no fee. 'What did Wrawe say of his fellow priests and of our lords and masters?' someone asked.

'The clergy just want to accumulate all; the aldermen and gentry raise taxation and re-elect themselves without considering the public good,' said Blackburn. 'All is done for the benefit of a few. They live sumptuously off our labours and they're extending their powers and eroding our traditional rights because they make the laws. These days, youths who have served their apprenticeships are denied their rights, for their masters make it near-impossible for them to be recognised as craftsmen and become independent. Instead, after years as apprentices, they are kept as mere hired labour at wages the king himself sets very low to please his cronies.

'In London,' the leech gatherer told his listeners, 'the master craftsmen and their apprentices are forming societies and leagues called guilds to get fair treatment. If one master mistreats his apprentice, all the members of that guild will refuse to work until matters are put right. When a child is born, the guild gives gifts to the parents; they help with hospital or funeral expenses, aid the sick or impoverished and do charitable work.'

19

At meeting after meeting in quiet churchyards or in the barn of a friendly host, Blackburn outlined the practicalities of forming a society. 'The lords of the manor must not know who organises us or those men will be singled out and punished. For now, as we form our societies, we let it be known we meet to hear Masses or to pray together. We keep our true plans secret!'

The meeting ended but most of those who attended had much to consider. Some of us went on to speak with members of established guilds and learned more. Each guild, because it restricts competition, is obliged to maintain good standards of quality to protect the public as well as to guard its own reputation, and new members must swear an oath (taken on holy relics) to that end. Bakers, for example, must use precisely specified types and quantities of materials to maintain the quality of their bread. Brewers must use only hops, grain and water in their ale; those who make bone handles must not trim them with silver to prevent the article being passed off as ivory; beadmakers must ensure their beads are perfectly spherical; candlemakers agreed to use four pounds of tallow for each quarter pound of wick; even the old-clothes mender must not press his refurbished garments to ensure they are not mistaken for new.

To enforce the strictures, guild officials make unannounced visits to check scales and inspect measures and generally pry and probe to see that all is as it should be to protect the customer. And there were other areas to police. Guild members may not attempt to create monopolies, nor can a retailer buy farm produce except at the weekend market when the farmer is actually present. The rule was designed to prevent the unscrupulous from doing private deals to corner the market in foodstuffs, for shortages are an ever-present threat and actual famine never remote.

* * *

The next time we met and spoke of creating a fellowship, a tall red-haired shepherd named Ralph Banton called for quiet. 'It's all right for you, Owen Blackburn,' he complained. 'You have no master and you have freedom to travel and can bargain for your work but we must deal with our lord on fixed, meagre terms and he wants more and more wool. Despite us working half the week for nothing, the king and his ministers encourage Zeelanders and Flemings to come here; they give them the pick of our lands and of our overseas trade. It's bad enough to pay these excessive wool taxes but it's worse to see strangers favoured over our own. These foreigners are not only taking the gold out of our country but they are also taking work away from honest Englishmen, who are starving.'

A rumble of agreement growled through the meeting. Strangers invited here to make us starve and take away our gold: this was surely cause to demand justice. A small man in a badly dyed green jerkin stood up. 'Our lords have no idea how hard our lives are,' he said bitterly. 'We must work like animals to bring in the crops and for no pay because the law says we owe work as rent for our miserable strips of land. We spent two weeks last year, women, men and small children alike, backs breaking, doubled over working with hand sickles to cut off the grain near its base. We had to pitchfork and turn it and stack it – and then it rained and rotted the whole crop. We near-starved last winter, living on cabbages and onions and rooting in the forest like pigs to find a few nuts. Did the baron care? He did not, feasting on venison as he was.

'Yet, three years ago,' Green Jerkin continued as his audience nodded In silent sympathy, 'Baric the skinner from Cuxton was caught with

21

a haunch of red deer. At the assizes in Rochester, he was convicted of poaching, branded on the face with a hot iron and hanged in the market square. All he wanted was to feed his family because the harvest had failed that year, too.' The group was silent, but the broth of resentment simmered.

I listened intently as the speakers went on to tell of the need for discretion, of how villagers met in their churchyards to form private groups, to elect their leaders, appoint night watchmen, or vote for wardens of a toll bridge. These elected officials improved their stinking streets and drained the alleys; they fined those who let their pigs run wild inside the village limits and they punished wrongdoers. Above all, they organised their communities and taught them to stick together.

The Bowerfield men heard some of the rules, agreed to their wisdom and resolved to form an association for mutual aid. We opted to create an archery society, reasoning that we were obliged by law to practise weekly in any case, but we also met occasionally in a corner of the churchyard. On such a day, Blackburn, who was becoming a sort of leader, advised us: 'The law also says each man must own a breastplate and a sword or spear. Keep yours sharp and stay in practice. One day it may come to violence if we must face down our lords.' A few of us made a mental note to do some sword practice at the pell, a pole behind the tavern where you could cut and thrust, as well as practising at the archery butts each Sunday.

All was not about crime or violence, though. Guildsmen from the victualling trade met rivals of the clothiers guild for wrestling or football or boat races on the river. As their numbers grew, said the preacher, so did their influence and power. Those guildsmen who banded together were no longer feeble subjects of their lords but could make successful demands for better pay or conditions. This I found very interesting and a scan of the crowd showed a few gaping mouths as others took in the revelations. We all knew at least by repute of the fat comfort of monks.

A salt boiler shouted to the scarecrow preacher: 'What about the church and its wealth from ground rents and tithes? Why do they not share that with the poor, instead of eating it all at their feasts?'

'Worse than that, brother,' replied the preacher, 'they have their own courts just for themselves and make us choose between the authority of our own king or that of their pope – and they can't even agree on having just one pope to fill the sandals of St Peter.'

Now it was my turn to gape. I had heard there were two popes, one in Rome or somewhere in Italy and the other in France. Our own priest was vague about it but the man was scarcely literate enough to do more than mumble some Latin he'd memorised without knowing its meaning. If the church was at war within itself, I thought, why did we pay such tithes to them? We might be giving to the wrong faction. We might not be buying our way into heaven after all. And, about those noble knights whose task it was to do the fighting: was it not true that humble archers had been shooting flat those highly trained nobles? At Dupplin Moor not ten years ago, 1,500 English archers had butchered a Scots force of knights and infantry ten times their number. It seemed the nobles who were specialist fighting men were no longer the best. Did they still deserve our taxes?

I looked around the crowd to find a fellow who might explain why there were two popes and which we should support when I saw three mounted men-at-arms cantering down from the manor. Someone

had reported the preacher's presence and the horsemen swiftly and
brutally took him away, snarling at the crowd to disperse, which
advice was quickly followed. But the scarecrow had done more than
defend a crop: he had already planted a seed...

Chapter 4

Flight

On Lady Day, in the year of Our Lord 1341, I killed my first man. The day was hard, bright and cold for late March, with daffodils and crocuses wavering in a chill wind. It was a lovely day of springtime promise and, for me, disaster.

A commotion near the tavern caught my attention and I saw two women running across the green, scattering squawking geese in their haste. Two men-at-arms were riding away, laughing, and I turned a corner to see they had dumped the scarecrow preacher half-naked on a dung heap. The women rushed to help him and I was drawn to go along myself, having an aversion to the bullying ways of Baron Roger's men.

As I arrived, one of the women clutched the other. 'He's badly hurt,' she said with a sob.

The tavern keeper heard the ruckus and came out to see what was happening. He assessed the scene and quickly hurried back inside to return with a cloak and a basin of water. The women produced pieces of linen and sponged blood from the fellow's battered face. 'He is a good man,' said one woman, white-faced as she cleaned the dirt and blood from Scarecrow.

'Does anyone know his name?' I asked. They shook their heads.

'Better tell our priest,' the other woman said.

'He'll not do anything,' said the tavern keeper bitterly. 'His living's in the hands of Baron Roger. Bring him into my tavern, put him by the fire and I'll send for the wise woman.'

I picked the man up and carried him inside, eliciting a groan or two from him but, to my eye, he did not look as if he would survive whatever had been done to him. One ear was half torn off, his mouth was a mess of blood and broken teeth and, to judge by his swollen right hand, his knuckles had been crushed. 'He's been tortured,' I said briefly and one of the women wailed.

The innkeeper reappeared, looking nervous. At his shoulder was a swarthy man in clothes of an unusual style who spoke English with a foreign accent. 'I can help,' he said simply, and I shrugged and moved aside.

He knelt by the injured man, hissed through his teeth, called for more linens and some hot water and began almost tenderly cleaning and binding Scarecrow's wounds. He was nearly finished when the village wise woman arrived with a steaming kettle.

'She told me he was hurt,' she said briefly, nodding at the goodwife who had brought her. 'This will help him sleep.'

Soon enough Scarecrow was peacefully asleep on a cot in the tavern keeper's own quarters. 'He has been hurt,' said the foreigner quietly. 'It is a wrong thing done to him.' I nodded agreement.

'Aye, our *seigneur*' – unconsciously I used the foreign term – 'is a harsh man. You have been kind, though.'

I eyed the foreigner's clothes: a knee-length tabard sort of tunic, a jewelled belt with a handsome scabbarded knife, a short cape over the shoulders. He caught my assessing look and smiled. 'I am Flemish. From Flanders,' he explained. I'd heard of it and knew it was somewhere near France. 'I am a trader.' The tavern keeper looked nervous and glanced over his shoulder. In the yard, I heard the stamp and snort of horses. The Flamand seemed to read my thoughts. 'Yes, young man,' he said. 'I have delivered wine for your Baron Roger and a little for your innkeeper, too.' He reached across the board and extended his hand. 'I am Francis and I bring good things to your country.'

Later, I would discover that our baron was involved in smuggling but at that time I was ignorant of an illegal wool-for-wine, wine-for-copper and copper-for-wool triangular trade between Kent, Flanders and Wales. It was a trade that one day would put a Welshman on the throne of England. Rustic that I was, I must have gaped, for the Flamand smiled. 'It is no secret among ordinary men who do not enjoy paying heavy duties to employ soldiers to kill each other in kings' wars,' he said. And, over a pot of cider, he explained the basics. English wool was highly valued for its long tough fibres but was taxed heavily at half a mark on a twenty-six stone sack. Wine from France was also taxed when imported to England. Welsh manorial lords whose lands contained slate and copper and who bred cattle for meat and hides also faced punishing taxes when they sent those items abroad.

So, the smiths of the iron-rich Weald of Kent who wanted to make amalgams for ploughs, tools, armour and weapons, imported copper (and slate for roofing high-prestige buildings and churches) and exported prized wool to the Flemish weavers. Their factors in turn sent wine to Wales or Kent and all the trading was done without alerting any royal tax gatherers. The Flemish wine ships put in unnoticed to small harbours along the southern coast of England, sailed around to Anglesey, in North Wales, to collect copper or slates, then made a return to Kent to trade for cargoes of wool which they discreetly carried home.

I sat in the smoky tavern cradling my wooden mazer of cider, listening intently as the trader smoothly explained his defiance of the lords of the manor and the king who wanted our customs dues. Until that memorable day, my thoughts had mostly been concerned with scraping a living despite all the regulations, tax demands, levies and dues. I was forbidden to forestall, regrate or engross my crops; that is, I was not allowed to buy up goods to sell when their price rose; I could not buy cheaply in hopes of making a profit and I could not try to create a monopoly, yet my masters could do all that and bleed their serfs white with taxes.

It was unlikely I'd ever become a trader. I had almost no coin and I was tied to my lord's land. Even if I grew surplus crops, our lords forbade peasants from buying grain in one market to sell elsewhere. They fixed prices low and confiscated a peasant's entire crop should he try to sell higher. Even the king demanded his right of 'purveyance' to buy grain at below-market price. Everyone seemed to profit, except those who did the work to grow the food.

Alfred the innkeeper arrived, wiping his hands on a cloth. He poured himself a mazer and sat down, comfortably companionable with the Flamand. 'Is Francis teaching you to defy your lord, Tom?' he queried me, grinning. 'You'd do better to take on the church; they're fatter geese for plucking. Our abbot owns much more than Baron Roger's got in his demesne.'

I raised my eyebrows. 'He has?'

Alfred swigged his cider. 'The abbot's got about two thousand acres in his benefice and he personally owns about a quarter of them.

28

He's got a fulling mill for cloth, two water mills where we are obliged to take our grain, a millpond, fishponds by the abbey, giant tithe barns, a brewhouse, a pottery, a smithy, a dairy and enough beasts to keep those fat monks in meat for years. All that, but even he is not as wealthy as the archbishop in Canterbury. He's got the income of dozens of abbeys, churches, chapels, chantries and preceptories to sustain his army of retainers in that huge palace!'

'What have you got, Tom? A half-acre, a sty for your pig, a few chickens and a hovel smaller than the abbot's feather bed, I wager. And it's the same for the other few hundred villagers who must live off beans and barley and hope it doesn't rain too much or at the wrong time, so you lose your crop and starve. Just be sure to hand over your tithes so the monks can continue to eat well.' He laughed bitterly. 'Who'd kneel in prayer for us if they starved to death?'

I walked home to our cot in thoughtful mood. The division of labour was unfair and the taxes were heavy but if I went to ask Baron Roger to improve matters, I risked a flogging for impudence. Worse still, Lizzie and I might be ejected from our holding and find ourselves tramping around the country seeking day work where we could.

As I approached our home, I spotted Lizzie spreading laundry to dry on bushes and called a greeting. She turned and came to me. 'A man was here for you. He said he'd come back soon.'

'Who was he?'

'I've never seen him before. He's not from the village.' Before I could ask more questions, a stocky dark-visaged fellow appeared from behind the hovel. He wore a thigh-length, buttoned cotehardie belted at the waist with a length of rope into which was thrust a heavy-hilted knife. 'I've been waiting on you,' he said brusquely.

'And you are?' I replied.

'Oliver the falconer,' he said. 'I work for the abbot.' And he spat copiously onto the ground.

Oliver. I'd heard the name during our muttered talks at the butts when we villagers grumbled about our work and poor treatment. 'I've heard of you,' I allowed, cautiously.

'And I of you, quarterstaff fighter,' he said with a twitch of the mouth. 'You're respected in this village. They say you're not just a stick fighter but you draw a good bow and could be a soldier.'

I ducked my head at the praise. 'I don't have a falcon,' I said innocently.

'Let us take a walk,' he invited. 'There are things we should discuss.' We shook hands. I told Lizzie I would be back shortly and we walked away. So, Oliver the falconer came into my life and changed it forever.

We walked along the bounds of the village and stepped into the forest where we would not be seen together, for what Oliver and I discussed we would not want our masters to hear. He proposed forming a guild or at least a secret society to band together and demand better pay for our work and better prices for our crops. 'If you can bring the reliable men of Bowerfield to a meeting,' he said, 'we can use the churchyard after dark – I'll fetch the men of Ashlea and Lowerthorpe and we can make a start at changing how we live.' For an hour we discussed plans; then I heard the swineherd's horn calling in his pigs and it was time to go, before curfew.

Oliver went one way through the growing dusk; I went another and, as I approached our hovel, I heard Lizzie cry out. I hurried my pace, emerged from behind the hedge and saw her struggling with a man wearing the livery of Baron Roger. I would know that shape anywhere. It was Ottercombe, the quarterstaff fighter I'd defeated. I rushed at him; he heard me and swung around, releasing Lizzie. 'Bastard,' I hissed, 'what are you doing?'

'Ah, just wanting a kiss from your woman,' he sneered. 'She's too good to waste on a peasant like you.' I smelled the beer on his breath and also saw he had his right hand resting on the hilt of a long dagger sheathed at his hip.

'I've got a fist here I'll share, if you like,' I snarled, and stepped forward. The dagger flashed out and gleamed dully in the poor light.

'Fist, eh? You rabbit, I'll gut you.' He sneered and slashed the dagger through the air before my eyes. I flinched away slightly, even as I drove my boot into his crotch. As he doubled over, I grabbed his hair in two hands, shoved his head down and brought my knee sharply up into his face. I heard the crunch as his nose broke.

That should have been all I needed to incapacitate him but even so, half-blinded and in agony from his crushed balls, he somehow lunged forward and thrust the knife at me. I took a slashing cut on my left forearm when I parried the strike, swung savagely with my right fist into the side of his head and the fight was over.

Ottercombe stumbled and folded sideways to his right. He groaned on hitting the grass, then in moments gave a sickening death rattle as his final breath exited his lungs. I stood there in disbelief, rolled him on his back and saw that he'd fallen onto his own knife. By a fluke, the long blade had gone in under the ribs and skewered him. I turned to see Lizzie, ashen, with her hands to her face. My head buzzed. I'd be hanged for this. My arm was pumping blood from a gash that looked like a bloody mouth. I stepped into the cottage and found a leather string. 'Tie this tight around my arm, Liz, just here,' I urged her. In moments she'd fumbled it taut. 'Now run and get the barrow.' While she went to the field, I dragged the soldier's body to the side of our home, out of casual sight. Mercifully, the dusk was thickening and nobody seemed to be about.

Lizzie returned with the barrow. I loaded my spade and the corpse into it and, grateful that I'd greased the axle with pig fat just a week ago so it ran quiet, went as silently as I could into the forest. Lizzie stayed indoors, talking loudly so it would seem as if I were home with her. In an hour it was done. I buried Ottercombe in a narrow trench I dug in the light loam, tipped him in sideways and stripped him of his valuables to make it seem like a robbery. I brushed the area with a branch to remove all traces of footprints, barrow marks and digging before I crept back home to have Lizzie sew up my wound with needle and thread.

I knew it was likely that animals would soon disinter Ottercombe but the missing valuables should divert suspicion from me. I waited until long after dark and went into our crop strips and buried the knife, purse and a silver chain that were all he had of value. Now I must conceal my wound and my discomfort…

Chapter 5

Outlaw

Ottercombe was soon missed and the lord sent other soldiers around the manor to question the serfs. Of course, after our quarterstaff bout and the complaints he had made about it to his fellows, I was a suspect and to Lizzie's fright two soldiers appeared at the half-door of our cottage to ask questions of me. No, I had not seen him, no, I had no idea of his whereabouts, he and I did not associate. One soldier grew weary of my intransigence and began wandering about the yard. I kept a wary eye on him and turned my body to conceal my left arm, where the bandaging under my tunic sleeve made the limb bulky.

As I moved, the soldier poking about outside called to his companion: 'There's blood here, Will!' A spatter from my slashed arm had fallen on some clean firewood during our struggle and we had missed it in the dark. Lizzie, who was sitting on a stool by the door while I was being questioned, turned quickly, rose, and walked to where the soldier was gesturing.

'Oh, that,' she said. 'I skinned a rabbit there the other day.'

Both soldiers looked suspiciously at her but she gave them a bright smile just as I said: 'And it made good eating, that stew.'

The visitors looked at each other; one shrugged and the other said darkly, 'We may be back.' With that, they trudged away.

Lizzie levelled a look at me. 'They suspect you,' she said quietly. 'It is time for you to be away from here my love, before they hang you.' We talked for an hour before deciding on a plan. Lizzie would stay to deflect suspicion and to say I had gone to collect a milk cow from her sister, who lived by the river Colne, near Colchester – a place distant enough to plausibly explain my absence for a week or so. What I actually planned was to make for Melton Mowbray, where I had cousins in the Brooksby clan. They would hide me for a month or so until matters had quieted and Baron Roger's suspicions and his interest in catching me were both, hopefully, waning. Lizzie would then slip away from Bowerfield forever and join me in Leicestershire.

'You know where we keep our coins hidden,' I told her. 'Alan Hardwick or the innkeeper Alfred will give you silver for any possessions you can't take. They won't fetch a good price but it should be enough to sustain you until you get to the Brooksbys.'

I decided to wait a few days before leaving to collect the fictional cow, thinking that would look less suspicious than vanishing immediately after being questioned, but matters did not work out as I hoped. A wild boar or other animal scraped up Ottercombe's grave and a peasant found and reported it. Three days later, a heavy rainfall sluiced away some of the tilth in my crop rows where I had buried the soldier's knife, belt and purse and two boys at play found the things and took them home.

By chance, my neighbour Hardwick, a good man and friend, was passing through the village when the boys arrived with their trophies. Although he did not recognise the knife and belt, he was astute enough to guess at their significance and came to warn me. In minutes, I had my cloak, knife, quarterstaff, pack with a few essentials including a pilgrim badge and some coins and was slipping through the dusk and out of the village. Much later I heard that the hue and cry had not gone out until the next morning, by which time I had taken a wherry across the Thames and was waiting at the gate of a priory with distinctive horn-shaped gables, for a breakfast served to the poor.

Being across the river meant I was well ahead of any pursuing hounds and I made my way north on the old Roman road of Ermine Street, keeping well away from Cambridge and Peterborough where the watch might be alert to me. I travelled slowly, for my wounded arm was infected and swollen and weakened me, but eventually I was passing the Hospitallers' hilltop leprosarium at Burton, almost at Melton Mowbray and safety. Then I was halted by five mounted, armed men who wanted to know my business.

I gave them a story about returning to Nottingham from a Canterbury pilgrimage and showed them the badge of St Thomas á Becket I'd won at dice from a drunken Kentish man years before. 'I saw the saint's holy bones,' I told them earnestly and they nodded at my devotion.

'And you are?' I asked. They stumbled a little over their explanation but I understood they were authorised by the Lord of the Peak, Sir Robert Tuchet and also had commissions from the prior at Sempringham and the abbot at Haverholm to retrieve goods stolen from their parishioners and from the religious themselves. 'And not all thieves are highwaymen,' said one sternly. 'We have corrupt king's men hereabouts, too.' I privately resolved to ask my kinsmen about that when I reached Melton. I bade the soldiers farewell as they wished me a safe travel, shouldered my pack and set out for Melton, where I was directed to my kinsmen's holding a few miles away in the hamlet of Frisby, on the meandering River Wreake.

The Brooksbys enjoyed a good piece of land as settled yeomen and made me welcome to their compound where my cousin Rodney answered my questions about the armed men who had stopped me on the road. 'We had an especially corrupt judge here a few years ago, Richard de Belers, a crony of the Despensers who were bleeding dry the royal treasury because the younger Despenser was the king's lover. De Belers was Baron of the Exchequer of Pleas, one of five royal judges and he enforced false judgements in the Despensers' favour, enabling them to sweep up vast estates and great wealth.

'He made the fatal mistake of threatening his neighbours, a clan called the Folvilles and, when he rode to dine with the Earl of Leicester, the seven Folville brothers and several allies from the la Zouche family waited in ambush by the river here. They shot his soldiers down, then ran De Belers through with a sword. As a result, the two clans were declared outlaws and put under the wolf's head – meaning they had the same status as a wild animal and could be hunted and killed without warrant. For all that, local people knew them as honest and law-abiding protectors against evil men and an oppressive judiciary.

'One son, Richard Folville is even an ordained rector of the church of the Holy Trinity at Teigh, near here.' Rodney paused and said quietly, 'When you heal, I think you should contact them and offer your services. They would welcome you and your weapons, for disputes here are too often resolved by force and you could use the safety the clan will afford you.' I winced at the 'when you heal', for I was only capable of watching a flock of sheep, not of the physical work I felt I owed for my keep, but the Brooksbys were kind. Rodney did me another service, arranging with a packman who was travelling to Kent to carry a message to Lizzie that I was well and would return soon, so she should stay. I had no qualms for her safety; she had relatives who lived not too distant and I needed to heal before I travelled south to face possible enemies.

At Rodney's suggestion, I met Eustace Folville, leader of the clan at their fortified manor house at Ashby and, as a lettered man able to read church and judicial records, I did what I could to help track down those who extorted money from the citizenry. I helped expose judges who took money from both sides in legal disputes and aided the unmasking of a fellow who pretended to be a royal tax collector. The rogue had no such warrant but simply lined his own pockets with the peasants' dues.

In time, disputes over territory and protection rackets arose with a clan of Coterels, who acted much as did the Folvilles to provide legally doubtful actions to recover goods for any who would hire them. The two groups even acted together once, when word came from Nottingham that a corrupt judge, Richard de Willoughby, who had seized land from the Coterels on a pretext, was coming to arrest us, and them. Eustace warned us: 'Willoughby is Chief Justice of the King's Bench while the king is away, but he does not act in the king's interest, only in his own. He has built great wealth by thievery, has estates in nineteen counties and manors in nine more, and has illegally seized mining and fishing rights. If he captures us, we will hang and he will strip our estates for himself. We must stop him.'

It took little time to form a plan to ambush the judge as he came from York on the Great North Way through Sherwood Forest. He must have believed his lofty rank would protect him, for he rode with just four men. They may have been enough to deter a highwayman but they were not enough to scare the Folvilles. The rector Richard was an expert archer and he shot two of the escort from their saddles before they could react.

We escaped into the great forest, where we held Willoughby for three weeks, chained to trees as we moved from camp to camp while his guards returned to York with a ransom demand. In time the money – 1,300 marks – came, to be handed over at an alehouse in the hamlet of Farndon on the banks of the broad River Trent.

Walter Folville collected the silver from two of the judge's servants, stepped quickly outside and was into a waiting wherry and pulling across the river before the servants could summon help. He was long vanished into the forest before the hidden soldiers who had accompanied the servants could gallop upstream to find a crossing.

Richard de Willoughby was released as promised but only after he swore a solemn oath of loyalty to the Folvilles. It was an oath he broke almost immediately. After only a couple of days, Willoughby pressured a Keeper of the King's Peace, Sir Robert Coalville, to raise the hue and cry for the Folvilles and a posse comitatus was gathered.

'They were too scared to come after us in the forest or here,' Eustace told us bitterly as we gathered at the fortified manor house in Ashby. 'So they went after poor Richard in his church at Teigh.'

Richard Folville was aware of the dangers he faced and had two sturdy workmen to help protect him. A skilled archer, he was described as 'savage and audacious' by Willoughby, so the justice sent twenty men to capture him. 'The skirmish went on for two hours,' Eustace told us. 'My brother barricaded himself in the church and shot dead one of Coalville's men and wounded several more. Eventually, Coalville persuaded Richard to come out of the church promising that he could leave in peace and speak his case before the king's justices.

Richard had little choice: his arrows had run out and his two fellow defenders were wounded. He chose to save them and walked out of his sanctuary unarmed.

'He trusted Coalville,' said Eustace bitterly, 'but the treacherous vermin seized him, beat him and hacked off his head in his own churchyard, without trial or absolution. I'll not finish this until Coalville pays for Richard's death with his own blood.'

The murder marked a change in the Folvilles and, although the Pope ordered that Coalville and his troops be whipped at each of the main churches in the region as penance for killing an ordained priest, the Folvilles sought revenge and became more violent. They began to care less about the common people and indulged more in looting, kidnapping, rustling and highway robbery. I took my share of the 1,300 marks ransom we had collected for the judge – it made a handsome sum which, at first, I protested was too much, but the brothers pointed out that I had worked with them for nearly a year and they were now taking more gold every week.

I left them without regret, eager to see Lizzie after my unexpected months away, and returned to Kent disguised under a heavy beard and a friar's cowled habit. Travelling light, armed only with my staff and a knife, I received handouts to a cleric for my food – it would have been suspicious for a friar to have the money I had hidden under my habit – and the trip went fast. Although I had been away from Bowerfield for less than a year, much had changed. The cottage that Lizzie and I had lived in was a charred ruin. Cautiously, aware that I faced hanging if I were discovered, I sought my friend Hardwick, making my approach to his dwelling in the dark, and after curfew. He was shocked to see me. 'Tom, we thought you dead!' he whispered, his eyes searching the night behind me for watchers as he ushered me into his home.

'Where's Lizzie?' I asked him urgently. He looked away.

'Tom, there's bad news, very bad news,' he said. 'Your Lizzie was found drowned in an abbey millpond. She rests outside the churchyard of St Michael's now – the clergy said she was a suicide and must not be buried in hallowed ground. We marked her grave with a white rock from the wall of her garden.'

My eyes blurred; my ears buzzed; my chest felt as if it held a cold stone. Lizzie was dead? She'd killed herself? That was impossible. 'Why did the monks say she'd done that?' I demanded.

Hardwick shook his head helplessly. 'They didn't say. They never share things. All I know is that someone came one night and torched your cottage. The village think it was soldiers angry about Ottercombe's death; his knife and belt were found buried on your strip of plough-land and of course you were not here so suspicion has fallen on you. It's all just a mess.'

My first thought was to go to the churchyard and view Lizzie's sad grave, my next was to walk away and leave Bowerfield and this part of my life forever. Hardwick seemed to understand my hesitancy. 'She's at rest, Tom,' he said gently. 'There is nothing here for you now. You should go. If they find you, Baron Roger will have you hanged.'

I shook my head. 'I'll come back one day,' I said thickly. 'The killing was an accident but, now, I just want to leave.' And I turned and walked into the darkness.

I walked all night, blindly unaware of my direction and, as the wolf light that precedes dawn lightened the sky, I found myself, dazed and drained, on the heights of the Kentish Downs. I stopped at a spring to drink and was overtaken by a group of dusty travellers who saw my friar's habit and badge and assumed that I, like them, was on pilgrimage to the shrine of Thomas Becket at Canterbury. They shared food with me and I trailed them that day and the next like a lost dog. In time we sighted the great towers of Christ Church and found the town, and even the cathedral close itself, swarming with Benedictines and the faithful as well as with the merchants who sold food, drink, plenary indulgences and fake relics to go with the badges which advertised the pilgrims' status. On instinct, I slipped away from my companions and sought the road south, the Portway to Dover. Some memory of a conversation with Lizzie told me to seek the Pope and get a pardon for killing Ottercombe. I also recalled my father telling me when I was a small boy that the Pope would require a payment for any service, so I paused and looked for an opportunity to acquire something.

It came as I passed an alley alongside the Parrot tavern and it took the form of a hawker of holy relics, a beefy character who eyed my cowled habit with its Becket badge and the slim purse slung from my belt and wheedled me: 'Holy brother, come and see these rare relics of Our Lord.' A glance around, a step into the alley, a look at the dross he offered ('These are the baby teeth of Jesus Himself') and a swift knock on the head with my staff was all it took. I had my relics and I took his purse, too, reasoning that he should pay penance for his impiety, and it would be convenient if the penance was not prayers but a practical donation to help a poor friar's mission.

I considered it wise to visit a barber who removed my heavy black beard and trimmed my locks before I visited a clothes stall and spent some of the hawker's silver on tunic, mid-calf braies and a good wool cloak to complete the disappearance of the wicked robber friar. And then I strode out for Dover. One of the two popes was in Avignon and I judged he could pardon my actions and extract poor Lizzie from purgatory. I even had his fee: Jesus' baby teeth. As I was travelling alone, it was wiser and faster to go by sea and not risk being murdered in my sleep when I journeyed across France. I'd take ship and sail around the danger, see the Pope and bargain with him to clear my sins. I'd also avoid being hanged.

Chapter 6

Voyage

Dover showed itself to me first by its castle and two stone towers, east and west. Once, they were Roman lighthouses that shone across the strait to a sister pharos in Boulogne. Today, one had been converted into a bell tower, but its strata of ragstone and red tile betrayed its origins and, when I got closer, I saw carvings of the old 'CLBR' for *classis Britannica* that the Romans used to mark property of their British fleet. The towers stand proud of the town, which sits in a river valley by tall white chalk cliffs that form the turf-topped southern battlements of Britain. Dover township is located where the shallow, tidal River Dour empties into the strait but the river is badly silted and its rundown quays and warehouses that stretch for a mile inland are largely idle.

Dover Castle makes an impressive locked doorway to England with a great keep protected behind inner and outer baileys where suspicious guards on the western Fitzwilliam's Gate surveyed me carefully as I humbly walked through. Inside the bailey was a crowded settlement with rutted, muddy streets where dogs, pigs and rats roamed. The place was piled high with rubbish and the chalk stream of the Dour was a shit-stinking sewer.

Because the river is largely silted up, the burgesses have excavated a pool and built new wharves where traders tie up and unload their cogs. This was where I hoped to find passage to France. The cargo-carrying cogs, clinker-built like their bigger brothers the hulks, have a pointed shape and, unlike the two-masted hulks, have just a single mast with square sail. The hulks tend to be more rounded and are steered with long oars over the sides while the cogs boast a stern rudder. They are used for shorter sea voyages and can flit across the strait to France or Flanders in a day. The largest vessels were Genoese carracks, flush-built, lighter and faster than their trading cousins. They came, I knew, from the Mediterranean and I eyed them speculatively. A passage on one of those galleys could take me speedily to the mouth of the Rhone, close to Avignon. I went in search of information and found a tavern where a pig-tailed Spaniard was drinking cider from a wooden mazer.

'You a sailor?' I asked politely and he nodded. 'Dangerous job,' I said and waved at his mazer. He nodded and the wench brought two drinks. He nodded his thanks and asked where I was bound. 'I'm off to France, to Marseille,' I said.

'A long journey and maybe a dangerous one,' he noted. 'I came from the Inland Sea last week and even at this time of year we had some bad weather.'

I asked politely what cargo he had brought and he told me it was the usual: sweet wine and dried lavender from the Languedoc plus a small consignment of precious spices and silks that had come via Genoa from the eastern lands, but he was more interested in discussing the hazards of a sea voyage. 'Which way will you take?'

he asked. I confessed ignorance and he sipped his cider and settled back comfortably, happy to display his knowledge. I sensed a dissertation approaching.

'Biscay's a problem,' he said, sucking his teeth. 'Going inshore, creeping around the coast of France and ducking into port after port seems safe but you'll face some dangerous sailing if the westerlies blow up. That is when the big waves pile up, steepen in the shallower coastal waters, slam against the coast and then wash back out. They create a maelstrom of fast tide rips that will sink you. It's better to go across the bay, taking the deep water and the big swells. See, there's deeps in the Atlantic that turn into shallows some thirty leagues out from the shore. They can make the inshore very rough with breaking seas and there's lots of treacherous undersea valleys and rocks to wreck you.'

He slurped his next draught and said moodily: 'The very shape of the bay is a trap. If you get caught with strong westerlies, they'll drive you into the armpit of France, under the outstretched arm of the land. It will embay you, and then there's no escape around Ushant, which is all rocky teeth and frequent fogs. If you choose to risk the coast route, you'll need at least four days of good weather before you get to the shores of Spain, where you'll be safer.

'Take the offshore route and you'll need at least six days of fine weather and that is only in the spring and summer months. You can only sail without much worry between Easter and St Luke's day and with even less worry if you pay three or four pence to your patron saint and make sure you travel only on a strong boat with a good crew.'

So that was what I sought, down in the wharves. After speaking to several masters and mates, I found no carrack available, so settled on a newish cog, the Saint Bartholomew, that was due to sail to Genoa in three or four days' time once its cargo of wool had arrived from Lincolnshire. It was about twenty-six paces long and ten wide and seemed a stout vessel, held together with iron bolts and square-headed nails as well as with the wooden pegs called 'tree nails'.

Although it had no deck as such, the master Rhys, a swarthy Welsh rogue with an earring and a missing eye, assured me that the canvas sail he would stretch across the cargo would keep out the seas. And, he added, the wooden superstructure at the stern he called an 'aftercastle' would provide good shelter. 'You'll sleep in there like a baby, my master,' he said, 'snug as a bug in a rug.' I viewed the low-roofed cabin mistrustfully, noted the four rough-planked cots and sighed inwardly. The master caught my glance and said: 'Aye, you'll not be alone. I'm taking three merchants with me to Genoa.' This would be an uncomfortable week or so. I just hoped for a swift voyage and that the winds were favourable. They were not, nor were my three companions in the small and smelly cabin good sailors.

Only hours after leaving Dover, an unexpected storm hurled us down-Channel and destroyed all hopes we had of making a safe, coast-hugging voyage around Biscay. Instead, the gale pushed us out into the open Atlantic. In an hour, everything we owned was soaking wet and to save ourselves we had to join the crew in a constant round of baling out water even while we were swooping sickeningly up and down the sides of spume-tipped, grey-green waves as tall as battlements. To add to the misery and fear that we'd soon founder, my cabin companions and even a couple of the crew were vomiting and soon were too weak to work.

The master grabbed my arm and shouted over the battering, howling

wind that I was a big fellow, I must help him get the sail in, for his
crew were fighting to control the rudder and reinforce the shrouds
before the mast was torn out. So, we struggled with gale-stiff canvas
that was as unyielding as rock. But our efforts were wasted: the sheet
split, streamed out ahead of us and tore itself free in ragged tatters
that immediately vanished downwind. With only a bare pole of a
mainmast to drive us on, our pounding speed eased, but the rocking
became more violent and one of the nine crewmen was washed over
the side, vanishing in an eye blink.

Night fell but the gale did not abate until a watery dawn came
with a few shafts of light, and we found ourselves enfeebled and
weary on a heaving ocean with no land in view. Conditions in the
cabin were foul. Because the ship's sanitation measures consisted
of two seats suspended airily alongside the bow, using them in the
rough seas we were enduring was suicidally dangerous. Instead, we
had a terracotta shitpot in our aftercastle to fill and add to the stink
and stench of vomit, urine and sweat, but it seemed an insignificant
trouble compared with our struggles to keep the Bartholomew afloat.
For two more days, weak, weary and nauseous, we fought our way
in a direction the master chose, sailing under a few scraps of canvas
and two sea cloaks that we employed as sails.

The one-eyed rogue knew his business, however, and brought us
one afternoon within sight of a great cliff. 'Cabo da Roca!' he said
exultantly. 'The rock of Lisbon! Now we are safe.' And we were.
Salt-stained and battered, stumbling from lack of sleep, we limped
up the River Tagus and found a berth in the harbour at Lisbon where
sympathetic port officials found us a corner of a warehouse where
we could sleep and brought us the first hot food we'd had in a week.

Owen the shipmaster traded a bale of wool for a stout, new

canvas sail and some hemp cordage and we cleaned and refitted the Bartholomew so we could resume our journey. Within a week we were sailing between the Pillars of Hercules on an easterly current of the Atlantic to enter the Inland Sea. I stood by the master as he watched the steersman. He was in relaxed mood now we had survived the storm and he wanted to talk. 'Came through here once when two of the sailors fought and one killed the other. The shipmaster ordered the traditional punishment: the killer was tied to the corpse and thrown overboard. There was no more knife fighting after that word went around.'

Our voyage, too, became tranquil. We passed the great port of Cartagena, staying well offshore against the possibility of the pirates who row out to intercept and board trading ships; we struck out north-east to Marseille and sailed in under a gentle breeze past the monastery and the ropemakers' walks into the Old Port first established as a trading post by the ancient Greeks.

I left the Bartholomew and its stench with relief, sniffing appreciatively at the salt air, and although I got a few curious looks for my ragged appearance, people also glanced at my size and my stout staff and looked away. There was a market in the city, a place where I washed and was barbered. I spent one of my gold coins on new boots, clothes and a good knife to replace the one I'd lost at sea and, suitably cleaned, went in search of a meal and a bed. I found both at an auberge called the Blue Cat and I also met there a fellow Englishman of my own age.

He heard my stumbling attempts to order food and came across the room. 'My name's Rob,' he said. 'Robert Knollys. From Cheshire. Can I help you?' He was a stocky, shortish twenty year old, with a clipped brown beard and cropped head, a contrast to my two clothyards of height, long black hair and clean chin. He spoke to the serving wench in some patois I did not know but soon a plate of viands appeared and all was well. Rob was, he said, in France for his lord, a northern nobleman, on a business that seemed mysterious. Rob dismissed it as only 'gathering information' but I soon found that he travelled with a dozen tough-looking Welsh and English archers including one called Christian who was just a fresh-faced boy. 'We need protection against highwaymen. We carry coin,' Rob said airily. 'That one there' – gesturing at one of the archers – 'is young Christian's half-brother and is all the family he has.'

Later, I would learn the boy was orphaned and had trailed along with his half-brother Anthony for lack of a place to go. I also found that Rob Knollys was spying for military purposes. His command of Latin and French, the language both of court and of the region where he was spying, had made him the choice of a great duke. 'I've been here for weeks,' he said cheerily, 'just looking at roads and bridges and things.' That 'just looking at' included mapping the terrain, roads and bridges, assessing supplies in the fields, sourcing wagons and recording where draught animals could be found. The intelligence would be invaluable a year or two later when Henry of Grosmont, the Duke of Lancaster, mounted great raids across France. Invaders do not assume that a weighty siege train can cross a bridge or ford a river. They scout the terrain first. This Knollys was a young man given large responsibilities and had the background and training to execute them well.

'Where are you headed, Tom?' he asked me. A little sheepishly I admitted I was going to Avignon to see the Pope, making no mention of murder or pardons. Rob assumed I was devout and raised an eyebrow but said thoughtfully he should look at the Rhone valley, too, and if

I did not mind, he'd accompany me, a group is safer than one, eh? So it was that I met Robert Knollys, a man who would be known to history as an infamous soldier and ravager, a man who became my close friend, my brother in arms and my betrayer.

Chapter 7

Avignon

On a quayside in Marseille, I met a trader who was overseeing the unloading of small barrels of a grainy black paste and asked him about finding a ship to travel the thirty or so leagues up the Rhone River to Avignon. 'Going there myself,' he said casually. 'On that.' He gestured at the trim cog from which the labourers were bringing the barrels.

'Got room for two passengers?' I asked.

'I will have when I've had these unloaded.' I feigned polite interest and he launched into an enthusiastic description of the *pastel* he grew north of the papal city. 'You can make fine blue dye from the leaves of little yellow flowers. I have a *moulin* – a mill – to shred and pound the leaves into pulp. I leave it to dry and ferment for six months, form it into a ball that would fill your hand, dry, crush and wet it again and get this black paste. It ages like wine and you get an intense blue colour. You call it woad.

'There's great demand for my dyes,' he said proudly.

Rob strolled up, understood my mission and interjected. 'Then you must be in a hurry to get back to your fields, eh?' The little trader

51

looked at Rob as if he'd popped out of the ground, eyed his appearance and evidently decided this was not a person to annoy.

'Are you travelling to Avignon, also?' he asked. Rob nodded and the trader said thoughtfully, 'It will be good to have two stout fellows to protect us.' He named a modest fare. 'We will leave in four or five hours, when the bells sound for Nones. That's when we'll catch the tide.' He viewed us again and decided it wise to question these possible pagans: 'You do know the sequence the monks use, from Matins to Compline?'

I nodded. 'Our carillons sound those calls to prayer, too,' I said. 'We'll be here after Terce and Sext but before Nones. In England we have those bells, which sound every three hours or so; we also have a goose bell at dawn to remind people to release their flocks to graze for the day and an evening pig bell to bring in the birds and release the swine to forage for the night.' The trader turned away to view the porters unloading his ship. He was unimpressed with our geese and pigs.

The journey to Avignon went well. Rob seemed to know things he should not, for he ordered his archers to locate a ship for passage and to wait for us in Venice, which puzzled me, but I did not query it. He and I left the Old Port of Marseille, sailed west along the coast, passing the marshlands of the Carmargue and its wild horses and entered the mouth of the great river Rhone. The wind was fair and we covered the thirty or so leagues a night and a day, coming in sight of the fine bridge of Saint Benezet, with its twenty-two arches, late in the afternoon. 'Most of the bridge was destroyed a century ago,' remarked the trader, 'and despite the church forbidding it, the people rebuilt it themselves, and they even improved it by raising the roadway above the original.'

Pope Clement's palace was inside the walls of Avignon. The previous pope had rebuilt it as a fortified cloister; the current occupant, the sixth Clement, had built a luxurious new palace with a Templar tower, a study tower, towers named for angels and gardens, a campanile, a dog tower and the tower of St Lawrence. There were other specialised buildings for kitchens, lavatories and an icehouse. We approached the gatehouse, explained our business, that we had a private message from Edward Plantagenet and a serjeant took charge of us after putting our weapons aside. 'Popes live well,' he smirked. 'Come and take a look.'

Rob snorted. 'You must know the saying: "To drink like a Pope?"' he asked our escort.

'You have to see the cellars,' said the serjeant. 'The clergy certainly don't go thirsty. Even the musicians the Pope brings in get so sozzled they sometimes can hardly play.'

The palace was a magnificent place: the 'chapel' could have been a small cathedral. More than fifty paces long, it boasted a vaulted ceiling so high and heavy it required the support of a vast flying buttress that stretched right across the neighbouring street. Frescoes decorated almost every wall; the floor was marble; the ceilings and pillars were splendid in blue, russet and gold leaf. The Apostle of Aquitaine, St Martial, was celebrated in a soaring chapel decorated with master-piece scenes of his life painted in vivid colours on all surfaces. The tombs of past popes, effigies of the great and good, armorial bearings in gold, crucifixions in both statuary and relief were everywhere, as were painted and plaster angels of all kinds and sizes. I caught Rob eyeing them speculatively and I fear I was agape, too. The serjeant was simply bored.

'This is a very grand room,' I remarked. 'Does the Pope sit in here all day?'

He shook his head. 'Too cold on some days; it takes forever to heat up. He prefers a day room – this one…' and he led us to the Stag Room, a papal dayroom painted lavishly with rustic scenes. It was large with a vast fireplace and a fine window that led onto a small balcony which overlooked the bridge and a jewel of a garden. 'His Holiness likes to get a breath of air out here and view the town and his flock,' said the soldier. 'He hasn't forgotten his roots as a lord.'

The Pope, a Benedictine whose true name was Pierre Roger and who was a nobleman's son from Limoges, had had a glittering career under the personal eye of Pope John XXII and, while still a young man, became abbot of one of the most important royal monasteries. In that role, he had been sent to summon our King Edward to France. It was him I had seen in Rochester as a boy: a pope-in-the-making sent on a mission which failed. We thought he was the Pope himself but that was still in his future. The serjeant coughed to get our attention. He was now done with us. 'His Holiness will send for you in a day or two,' he said, and took us to an army barracks block to settle in and wait.

'I talked to some people yesterday,' Rob said as we laid out our few belongings, 'and they told me this pope makes his relatives high officials of the church. He has made cardinals of three nephews, a cousin and five cronies from his home region: there's only one Italian in the entire cardinalate. He's a nepotist who consults astrologers and he's likely highly corruptible. You'll get your pardon if you can pay.'

Well, I couldn't. With dismay, I assessed matters. I had a small supply of gold and my best bribe was that I had the fake relics of the teeth of Christ. It seemed I'd not found a charitable prelate, just a greedy one. I needed to think.

Inspiration came that evening as Rob and I sat in a tavern drinking watered French wine. A handsome gypsy woman came by selling 'holy' charms and relics to pilgrims. I coaxed her to sit with us and slipped a couple of coins into her welcoming hand. 'I have more: two gold pieces for you,' I said, 'if you can carry out a simple task…' We spoke for an hour, rehearsing her duties until I was convinced it was possible. An error might mean both of us could be incarcerated but the idea should well work. I arranged for her to wait nearby the next day, or even two if needed, but the summons to the papal chamber came as expected late the next morning and I told the messenger to wait while I prepared myself for the noonday audience. Rob had made his arrangements and slipped away to the little garden under the Pope's window; I gave the gypsy a written message to show the guards and she hurried away.

Within an hour, I was standing in the Stag Room. Pope Clement was sitting on an ornate throne and I approached humbly, bent and kissed the ring he extended, a gold circlet showing a bas-relief of St Peter fishing. Now, I was the fisher of a Pope. An oily prelate interpreted my words at first but the Pope waved him away and spoke in good English. 'You have a message for me from your king?' he questioned. 'The same Plantagenet who would not answer my lord king's summons to his vassal?' I glanced nervously at the oily prelate, and Clement, reading my meaning, curtly dismissed him from the chamber.

'Thank you, your Holiness,' I said, stalling for time. 'My mission is highly confidential and…'

A discreet tap on the gilt door interrupted us and a majordomo slid into the chamber. 'Am I not to have quiet?' Clement demanded.

'This, Holiness, is important, very important.' He sidled up the throne and whispered in Clement's ear, then handed over the scrip

I had given to the gypsy woman. Clement read it and straightened up abruptly.

'Bring her to me,' he said. 'Be sure she is not carrying a weapon.' Two men-at-arms escorted the gypsy into the chamber and she knelt before Clement. 'Is this true?' he asked her, waving the paper.

'I did not write it, lord,' she said. 'It was written for me by a friend who loves you. After I looked into the future and told her my fears, she said I had to deliver the note to warn you.'

Clement went pink. 'You looked into the future?'

'Yes, lord, I can do that.' Her face was so clear and pure that even I believed her, and I knew she was lying.

'What did you see?'

'It does not seem to make sense, Holiness. I saw a man whose teeth will protect you.'

Clement stood up. 'Is this a joke? What is this nonsense, that some man will save me with his teeth?'

'They will not be his teeth, lord,' the gypsy said. 'They will be holy teeth.'

I exclaimed aloud. 'Holy teeth, you say? Who has been telling this woman things?' He looked at me, puzzled, but his curiosity and his superstition overcame his doubts. This was a man who consulted astrologers.

'What things?' Clement demanded of me.

I came back with a rejoinder: 'How does she know of the Plantagenet gift? It is all supposedly secret!'

Clement looked rattled. 'Be clear with me. What gift have you?'

With a show of reluctance and some sideways glances at the gypsy and the vastly interested guards, I pulled a wrapping of fine linen from my purse. It bore some embroidery a woman at the tavern had carried out the previous night, the initials ER. '*Eduardus Rex,* your Holiness,' I said. 'These came from Constantinople when the crusaders ravaged it. They are the baby teeth of Christ. My king sends them as a token of truth.' I had my back to the window and its small balcony; the teeth and their wrapping were in shade in front of me.

Clement crossed the carpet to take the package from me and stepped to the window to view it in better light. I stepped forward, saying urgently: 'No, your Holiness!' and I put my arm in front of him, shielding him at the exact moment Rob's beautifully aimed arrow clattered harmlessly off the stonework. The next quarter hour went by in a blur. Rob removed himself swiftly from the little garden below; the guards seized me; the gypsy appeared to faint and Pope Clement farted loudly in fright.

When matters settled, the gypsy explained she had foreseen the incident and my actions, realised she would never gain an audience, had a note written in hopes it would be delivered and had been surprised to be present to see yet another of her prophecies come true. In a matter of minutes, she was reading Clement's palm and telling him of a glittering future; I was being congratulated on my action saving the successor of St Peter and I was promising to do anything to show my gratitude if the Pope would grant me a pardon for what was, after all, just a mere accident. I did not stress that it had cost Ottercombe his life.

Clement looked thoughtful and said for my penance I must take the Cross and go on crusade. 'You can go on a holy mission to Smyrna and help bring the Turkish pirates to heel. You can join the Venetians, who are putting together a fleet of galleys and you can earn your indulgence by keeping Christian sailors safe.' He turned to the gypsy woman who, I noticed again, was very handsome. 'And you, my child, can come with me away from these people to help predict my future.' She looked helplessly at me and I thought, well, the Pope has more gold than I do, so she'll probably do better with him than getting just two gold pieces from me. I almost had my pardon and my soul would be saved. I could go to heaven. First, however, I must go to war.

Chapter 8

Venice

The spires, domes and towers of Venice gleaming in sunlight were a sight to take away your breath and we sailed into the sparkling lagoon before a stiff breeze on which a flock of screaming gulls wheeled and dived. Rob slapped my shoulder as we stood admiring the views. 'Looks like quite a fleet,' he said, indicating a forest of masts in the shelter of St Erasmus' Island. 'They say the king of Cyprus is leading this crusade; the Pope has ordered the men of Venice and the Knights Hospitallers to take part and we get all of our sins forgiven for joining in.'

Pope Clement was the power behind this venture to sweep the Turkish pirates from the Aegean Sea, a venture he had expanded after two predecessor popes' efforts had proved to be ineffective. Popes John and Benedict had maintained a squadron of four war galleys to protect Christian shipping but far too many of the church's flock were held as slaves, chained to the oars of heathen galleys or kept as playthings in the seraglios of the emirs. Clement called a crusade against the Emirate of Aydin and its ruler Umur the Lion and had already defeated a small Turkish fleet in a sea battle because the emir had failed to send many of the 350 ships he commanded. The Pope decided to seize the strategic port of Smyrna that controlled the Aegean coast and base Christian war galleys there.

It was not to be. Days after we landed in Venice, word came that the advance force had captured the citadel at Smyrna and our crusaders were needed elsewhere, at the Crimean city of Caffa which was under siege by the Mongols. Their 'Golden Horde' was a huge Islamic army which had emerged from a khanate that stretched from Siberia to the Black Sea, from the Caucasus to the Carpathians. They occupied the southern Steppes, which was good land for horses, but they turned away from the forests and swamps to the north and swept across Europe through Spain to Arabia, a conquering, pillaging force of Turks and Mongols. For all that havoc, they knew the value of commerce and deliberately left trade caravans unmolested.

'We and others in the Mediterranean have dealt peacefully with them for eighty years,' explained a Venetian merchant who sold Chinese silks and Baltic amber. 'At first there was agreement and we built Caffa on a tributary of the Don where it meets the Black Sea. There, our great Genoese galleys met with trading vessels that sailed down the Don from Russia and also linked with the caravans that bring goods from China along the Silk Road which ends at the sea.'

Things went wrong, he told us, because the Genoese who'd bought the site from the khan of the Golden Horde established a large slave market at Caffa, traded in captured Turks and sold them as slave soldiers – mamluks – to the Arab sultans of Cairo. The khan was angered, for the slaves were his subjects. He ordered the traders arrested and laid siege to Caffa, which is sited at the foot of the peninsula of Crimea. After a year or so the Genoese burned their town and retreated. They returned only after the khan died and his successor allowed them back. The Genoese rebuilt Caffa as a citadel behind two strong concentric walls between square stone towers and it flourished to become a place of about 17,000 people.

The rebuilt city had fine markets, wide streets, a harbour crowded with about two hundred vessels and a cosmopolitan population of Genoese, Kipchaks, Alans, Jews, Armenians, Greeks and Mongols, each with their own quarters. A special, walled section of the city was occupied only by merchants who could bar their section's gates for extra security.

The Venetian merchant, a *consigliere* of his city-state's elected duke, the doge, told a war council of crusaders that there was another enclave of Italian merchants sited at the mouth of the Don River in an ancient trading place called Tana. There had been a brawl between the Christians and Muslims there; blood was shed, a Muslim died and the Italians fled to Caffa. The Mongol chief demanded that the Christians hand over the killers; Caffa's leaders refused and the Mongols decided to finally rid themselves of all these troublesome Christians and returned to the walls of Caffa with siege engines.

'The Holy Father wishes us to delay our crusade to Smyrna and go urgently to the relief of Caffa,' said the doge's official, 'so our force will join the Venetians and sail for Caffa.'

Rob Knollys, sitting beside me, muttered: 'If the defenders have access to the sea we could be in good shape. A siege won't work if the defenders can be resupplied. It's supplies, not tactics that win conflicts.' Although I was the older, Rob had been tutored in the skills of war and had been appointed as a captain of the Pope's force.

I tugged at my beard to help me think, then ventured: 'If there are as many of these Mongols, Tatars and the rest that I think there are, they may well make it difficult for us, but we'll know more when we get there.' And we did.

Our flotilla sailed into a fine wide bay to find Caffa was a well-built port nestled under the protection of two sturdy fortresses on the headlands above it. The forts' curtain walls were protective enough to allow us to sail right into the harbour unmolested, although we were so close to the besiegers, we could easily view their siege lines. Their fortifications and distinctive yellow felt tents wrapped part way around the town in a crescent. Smoke from the Tatars' cooking fires rose in the calm air and we could clearly view an array of rock-throwing mangonels and trebuchet engines; also, wheeled towers called belfries that allow attacking archers to fire down on the defenders. These towers included a drawbridge that could be dropped so attackers could rush across it onto the defenders' battlements. There were also rams, catapults and a zigzag ditch that menaced the walls but not a single missile was fired at our squadron of ships, and we disembarked and unloaded in perfect safety before marching into the citadel through the port gate.

'That was easy,' said Rob, sniffing appreciatively as he caught whiffs of cooking, 'but there do seem to be plenty of the enemy.' We had met a grizzled Genoese mercenary who had command of a section of wall and climbed with him up a stairway onto the ramparts of the outer bailey. He gestured at the sprawling encampment that spread before us for more than a mile.

'About 25,000 men,' he said authoritatively. 'But they've no ships. They're mostly horse soldiers, not infantry, not sappers. They can't prevent us being resupplied so they're wasting their time. They can't win this one however they try.'

But try they did. To breach the walls, the Mongols brought up ever-larger throwing machines, engines so heavy they had to survey and reinforce the roads and bridges over which their teams of oxen dragged the monster catapults. They broke up buildings to use the stones as ammunition; they cut down acres of forest for the baulks of timber they needed to build or repair other engines.

Foraging squads went out for miles to bring in cattle for food and for their hides, which were needed to make replacement slings to hurl the stones, for a trebuchet could wear out two large slings a week. The Mongol khan Jani Beg set saddlers to cut and sew the slings and sent across the Black Sea to Constantinople to recruit ropemakers to create cordage. He put blacksmiths from his armies to work producing the ironware the Mongols needed to build siege engines and create or repair weapons, tools and armour.

Those smiths needed charcoal to heat their forges, so Tatar axemen and foresters were sent to harvest timber and to build and tend the mounds of turf-sealed wood fires that created the high-temperature carbonised fuel. The artillery also had needs: for quarrymen, stone cutters and masons to cut and shape the great stones they'd hurl from the biggest engines, which would throw two hundred or more shaped missiles each weighing 50lbs every day.

But the greatest need was ours. We required bolts for the crossbowmen and arrows for the archers. I am no fletcher but, along with other archers, I spent hours and days retrieving spent arrows and using their flights on new shafts of ash, beech and even pine. When we had supplies, I took my place on the fighting platforms of the battlements and poured shot after shot into the besiegers: so many shots I could feel my accuracy and strength improving by the day.

* * *

Some of the Mongol archers used armour-piercing arrows made of bone but they were only truly effective at close range. For us inside the walls, we used missiles. Our defenders equipped with Genoese crossbows or the English mercenaries with longbows whom my cousins had joined could shoot down an armoured man at two hundred paces if they used a bodkin-pointed, clothyard arrow. The Genoese, mindful of the previous Mongol siege of their city, had laid in a plentiful supply of quarrels for their crossbows and each arbalester had two loaders to keep his weapons charged. The English archers were more lethal. We could, unaided, fire six clothyard arrows a minute – a rate of fire which meant that a relatively small number of archers could create a storm of steel slamming down from the sky. But even the slow-loading crossbows could be deadly.

Rob said casually: 'If we have just two hundred arbalesters, each firing a leisurely four bolts an hour, the enemy will be receiving thirteen shots a minute. That's near-constant fire: an incoming bolt every five heartbeats. It's enough to make them keep their heads down and, even if they do, they'll still take casualties who will need their comrades to carry them to the rear. Unrelieved fire disrupts everything but it does mean we'll need a lot of missiles.'

I queried his calculations. 'Fact,' he said briefly. 'I fought at Sluys in a naval engagement and saw the damage archers can do. Also, my father was at Dupplin Moor when the longbowmen slaughtered the Scots King David's armoured knights. He told that story so often and in such detail, I almost feel I was there. I was only a boy but I've never forgotten those descriptions.'

Chapter 9

Siege

The Genoese garrison knew their business and used the mural and corner towers to great effect, pouring enfilading fire into the flanks of the Mongols who were labouring to lever up the wheeled belfries and rams. The former of these, when dragged up close to our walls, allowed their archers firing platforms higher than our ramparts, while the rams, under their sheltering roofs, could batter at the walls with swinging, iron-tipped great baulks of timber.

From time to time, a wave of enemy infantry would race across the open ground with scaling ladders in vain attempts to escalade the walls, but our archers were too accurate and few ladder carriers survived the hail of missiles that flailed them. A handful of times, Mongols got over the walls and, on one occasion, when my sword broke, I actually killed one enemy with a spear butt I used as a quarterstaff by jabbing him through the left eye, bursting it and penetrating his brain. That night, I met two of my cousins who'd travelled to Caffa with me and proudly told them of my action. Joseph shrugged. 'We're fighting with the professionals, the mercenaries from Wales and Cheshire.

They can put an arow through a Mongol's eye at a hundred paces.' I humbly ceased my boasting.

During attacks, the enemy bowmen had great difficulty hitting our archers with return fire because the Genoese had fitted hinged flaps between the merlons of the battlements. Our archers raised the boards to fire from behind the protection of the crenels, then ducked back behind the dropped flaps to shelter while they reloaded. A few used civilians or boys to raise the flaps, then two archers would fire simultaneously before stepping back as the board was dropped back into place.

While this action was happening, Turkic sappers were digging a covered zigzag trench towards the walls of our outer bailey, changing direction from time to time so we could not shoot down the length of it. The diggers at the head of the trench worked behind the protection of a cage of rocks and we watched carefully to gauge when the sappers would change direction and move the protection. Each time, it gave us vital moments that allowed us to fire directly into the diggers.

Rob was watching the steady advance of the trench with approval. 'They're good,' he said. 'If we don't make a sally and destroy their work, they'll be in position to bring up petraries and hurl rocks at us from very close range. The same goes for those belfries. If they can haul them closer, we'll have trouble holding this outer wall as they fire down on us.'

The Genoese commander must have had similar thoughts, for soon we saw work parties dragging pots and containers up to the ramparts where our own catapults were firing. 'Greek Fire,' said Rob with satisfaction. 'It's a devil's brew of saltpetre, pitch, resin, sulphur, bitumen and some other things. Ignite it and hurl it – the stuff clings and burns through almost anything.' Soon enough, the stink and smoke from the brew caught my attention and I watched as a crew gingerly loaded a smoking terracotta pot into the sling of a mangonel, then hurriedly stood back until the operator released its swinging arm and ducked away.

The pot arced through the air, a small dot travelling lazily, then smashed onto the ground close to one of the belfry towers, spewing sticky fire towards it. 'Missed,' said Rob, 'but close.' The second pot also fell short; the third did not, shattering on one of the belfry's huge crosspiece timbers. Nothing seemed to happen for several minutes; then a curl of smoke rose and a bright finger of flame began to crawl up the structure. In moments, the flame grew larger and the men below who were levering the tower across the ground turned and ran. The dried-out timbers caught with remarkable rapidity and, in just minutes, flames were travelling across the whole edifice. Frantic Turks tried to organise a bucket chain to douse the growing fire but their efforts were disrupted by our archers, who skewered the hurrying figures. We watched as the entire belfry was wrapped in flames before it lurched and crashed to the ground in a bonfire whose heat we could feel from a hundred or more paces' distance.

A crunching sound to my right caught my attention and I saw a small landslide of rock and mortar slide down the side of one of our corner towers where a mangonel's missile had struck. I turned to view the engine: a construct that looked like a child's see-saw. It was a beam, about fifty paces in length, pivoted on an axle placed at about a quarter distance along its length. On the shorter end, a stoutly built wooden box contained, said Rob, nine or ten tons of lead and rock. 'The longer end is drawn down to the ground by a windlass. That end has fastened to it a long sling made from cowhides. The operator loads a heavy stone into the sling then releases the windlass. The weighted box slams to the ground; the sling whips viciously fast and accelerates the rock it holds into a high arc and onto its target.

'It's good when it works but the box containing the weights can only take so much pounding; the winch that drags the firing arm down needs to be massively strong but must release easily; the cowhides fray and break and the whole thing must be greased with tallow and pig fat to keep everything working properly. It's a constant struggle to keep these engines operating.'

Struggle or not, the hours were punctuated by the thump and hiss of the Mongol mangonels as they sling-shotted huge rocks at our fortifications. In counterpoint, we defenders hammered, chopped and sawed baulks of wood and chiselled and mortared timber and stone we took from ruined houses to repair the gaps the siege engines had made. And for a week or more, things seemed to be at a stalemate. Then, one dawn, an alert sentry reported strange happenings at the entrance to the sappers' trench.

'The Turks seem to be carrying small trees in there,' he told his officer.

At the morning war council, the officer made casual mention of it, with: 'They must be getting cold; they're dragging fuel into their rat holes.'

The Genoese commander, Silvio Sanpietro, knew better. 'What sort of fuel? Describe it!' he said shortly. The officer could not, so he sent for the sentry, who described stout poles about the height of a short man and of the thickness of his leg at the thigh.

'They are pit props,' Sanpietro declared. 'They are undermining our walls.' From the battlements, Sanpietro pointed out half-concealed heaps of dirt that were lighter in colour than the ground around them. 'They must have brought out that spoil at night, unobserved. They probably have a good-sized cavern excavated already, judging by the size of the heaps, and because those timbers are not for fuel, they're props to hold up the cavern roof. We'll have to act quickly.'

Spies told us that the Mongols had recruited Anatolian silver miners to dig under our walls. Their plan was to use wooden stanchions to prop up the roof of the cavern we guessed they had dug under our outer bailey wall, a cavity they would fill with inflammable material – King John famously used the fat of forty pigs when he undercut the gatehouse at Rochester Castle – and they would soon set fire to it. The miners had dug several venting tunnels through the cavern walls to the outside. These would create a through-flowing blast of air that would fan the fire to a raging blaze; the wooden props would burn through; the roof would cave in and the wall above it would crumble into the hole, creating a breach in our defences through which the Golden Horde's warriors could pour into the stronghold.

Unless we could stop their miners, we were doomed.

Knollys questioned Sanpietro closely. 'These venting tunnels: how big will they be? How many will there be?'

The Venetian shrugged. 'I do not know but they must be big enough for miners to kneel in them to dig through to the outside and I'd expect them to excavate at least six.'

Knollys looked thoughtful. 'If a man can dig them, other men can access the cavern from the outside through them. How long will they be?'

Sanpietro shrugged expressively. 'How deep is the cavern? Our walls are high, they would want a deep hole into which to collapse them. Maybe the air vents are thirty or forty paces long. We do not know.'

Knollys looked at me and said deliberately, 'We're going to have to find out.'

It was not as difficult as I imagined. That afternoon, Rob and I took a handpicked squad of men-at-arms, instructed them carefully and we began a close examination along the ground inside our battlements. We knew the Mongols wanted to collapse the wall, so the hole must be directly below our defences. While a desultory exchange of missiles went on from the battlements above us and carriers trotted past with bundles of bolts and sheaves of arrows in willow-wand-stiffened linen bags to prevent the flights from being crushed, we scoured the ground inside our wall.

One of Knollys' Welsh archers found it first: a weed-covered wooden hatch that concealed the entrance to a sloping tunnel. Twenty-two paces away, a similar hatch was spotted by another man-at-arms but the two air vents were all we found. 'The others are probably outside the walls,' we agreed. At dusk, a half dozen of us slipped out of a sally port and began combing the ground. We found one more ventilation tunnel, plugged with a bale of straw and disguised under broken tree branches. We left it intact, as we had also left the two hatches, but marked the spot and retreated, hopefully unseen.

By morning, we had rigged two large blacksmith's bellows beside the two tunnel mouths that were inside our wall and we had assembled a woodpile, several three-gallon tubs of oil and a good quantity of bitumen, sulphur and pitch. We enlarged the two entrances somewhat and built an oil, sulphur and bitumen-soaked fuel stack in each hole. Then, wearing damp masks over our mouths and noses for protection, we capped the stacks under alternating layers of damp sand and canvas and set them afire. The bellows, whose extended nozzles we inserted under the canvas, blasted air into the fuel heap and forced its dense smoke into the tunnels. As we hoped, the Mongols' roofed sap trenches acted like a chimney, dragging the sulphurous, tarry fumes into the cavern to blind and choke the miners inside. In a short time, they began staggering out, gasping for air. They made easy, stumbling targets for the archers and arbalesters we had massed on the fighting platforms above us. In an hour, as their targets came out blind as moles, our bowmen and crossbowmen shot down fully one-fourth of the Anatolians who had been tunnelling under our wall. We later learned that a considerable number of the survivors had eye and breathing problems that took them away from the mine for weeks.

When the smoke eased, a dozen Genoese volunteers wriggled down the vent tunnels into the cavern and removed, destroyed or damaged as many of the miners' discarded tools as they could find in the empty chamber. Some of our raiders buried poisoned caltrops in the dirt of the cavern floor and tunnels to spike and infect any who crawled in to reclaim their diggings. 'That,' said Rob Knollys, who was increasingly involved in strategic planning with the Genoese military leaders, 'will set back the siege for a while. They'll have to wait for their smiths to make new pickaxes and the like and until their captains can persuade new miners to venture into the tunnels again.'

As he spoke, horns blared and we rushed to the battlements to find swarms of Mongols attempting escalades, with a dozen ladders somehow already against our walls. Genoese soldiers began hurling down the rocks we'd gathered against such an attack, returning missiles the Mongols had catapulted into our bailey. The stones stripped lines of invaders from the ladders; defenders were pushing other ladders away with spears to topple them backwards into their comrades and there was a constant shouting for archers to pour arrows into the crowds at the foot of every ladder. I took a longbow and quiver from a dying archer and fired shaft after shaft into the attackers.

Some splintering noises caught my attention and I ran to the parapet to lean dangerously out and see what was happening. The sounds came from the area before the eastern land gate. Mongol axemen were hacking at the timbers of the portcullis and a horde of them was wheeling a battering ram into place. I heard huge cracking noises and ran towards the gate, shouting for soldiers to follow. Mongol arrows clattered around us but none hit and the half dozen men with me reached the gatehouse unhurt. I stumbled down into the chamber above the gate to find four men calmly boiling water and sand over several braziers. 'About ready,' said one, as he and his mate used a makeshift stretcher to lift an iron pot from the brazier. 'This one's for the drop box. T'others will be hotter for any of those devils that get through the portcullis.'

The stretcher bearers staggered across the flagstones, eased the pot onto a lip and poured the boiling sand and water mix through an open chute directly above the portcullis. Its arrival on the mob below was greeted with screams of pain and, almost simultaneously, with a rending noise as the portcullis shattered and was snapped from its grooves. I glimpsed injured and dying Mongols on the pavement; then more swarmed into the entry between the double gates. 'Time for the murder holes,' said one sweating soldier as he levered a stretcher's handles under the lip of a second iron pot. The dispatch and delivery of that consignment of blistering sand and water through a square hole in the gatehouse upper floor was greeted with even louder screams and, after a third boiling potful was poured through a murder hole, the Mongols retreated, leaving their scalded wounded writhing on the stones of the gateway.

Further along the curtain wall, the Genoese had repelled the attack and Sanpietro was organising a company of archers and spearmen to dash out from a sally port to hit the retreating enemy in flank. 'When they run, destroy that belfry!' he shouted, gesturing to an archers' tower which had been hauled close to our walls. Knollys spotted me with a dozen Cheshire archers who had run with me to the defence of the gatehouse. Among them was Knollys' bowman and his young brother, Christian, who was carrying two spare quivers of arrows. Rob waved me over and I joined the force as we gathered hidden behind a covering wall parallel to and protective of a gate. A handful of the Italians were carrying smoking firepots; a couple of dozen crossbowmen, each with one foot on the cocking stirrup, were winding up their cables and the Cheshire men were notching arrows and adjusting their loaded quivers. At a hand signal, we slipped out silently from behind the wall and loosed four volleys into the flank of the retreating Mongols. All they heard was the hiss of the missiles and the screams of their comrades, and they ran, leaving a tidemark of dead and dying.

It took just minutes to set fire to the timbers of the belfry tower and to slash the ropes of two mangonels before the Mongols mounted a tentative counterattack, but we moved swiftly to safety, arriving untouched inside our walls as the belfry went up in great tongues of fire, sparks and smoke. In the confusion, I did not notice that the young blond boy Christian was missing and assumed he had stayed with his Cheshire comrades. It was not until several hours later, when the fighting ended, and Knollys came looking for him that I realised he must have been left behind and was probably dead or a captive. One of the archers said he'd seen the boy's older brother killed by a spearman. 'We tried to get to the body but we couldn't – there were dozens of Mongols coming at us. It was all we could do to escape,' he explained.

We were a gloomy set of archers that night, for the grizzled mercenaries had taken to the diffident young boy and adopted him as a mascot, but life and the siege had to go on. Our commander set a small force of men to divert water from the small mountain lake Kafa that powered our watermill. They directed the stream down the air shafts and flooded the cavern, soaking the wooden props and making them difficult to burn. 'They'll have to start over,' said Sanpietro with satisfaction, 'but now we know their tactic we can destroy their tunnels before they get close.'

Chapter 10

Battle

Word came that Pope Clement, who had called for a crusade to halt pirate depredations against Christian ships, had diverted even more would-be crusaders to the relief of Caffa since the force already in the pirate stronghold of Smyrnia had captured the citadel, although the keep remained in the corsairs' hands. Each day now, galleys and cogs laden with men and supplies arrived in our harbour and the stronghold swarmed with armed men. 'We need 'em all,' said Rob Knollys grimly. 'There's probably 25,000 besieging us; they're the dog and we'll be only the tail until we get more reinforcements. It's good that we have strong walls and that the Mongols are really just horse soldiers, not artillery or foot, but it wouldn't take much for them to throw a mass escalade over our walls before we have the numbers to repel them.'

So, we stayed within our defences, sallying out occasionally on raids to wreck the Mongols' siege engines or kill their sappers and tumble their trench walls. The enemy seemed almost half-hearted about matters and did not always replace the towers and catapults we ruined. In the early days of the siege, they had built sturdy wheeled galleries shaped like huts. These roofed engines contained battering rams that swung to and fro inside them. The strong roof protected the soldiers manning the rams and repelled rocks and missiles hurled down from the battlements above. After we rained down fire, they simply covered the roofs with wetted cowhides that would not burn, but in time the enemy seemed to lose heart and simply let their abandoned engines be destroyed.

Even the missiles that had once caused panic and destruction came less frequently and as our inner bailey enclosed 6,000 houses, or about half of what the outer bailey also enclosed, damage from the catapulted rocks was tolerable and people helped each other if their homes were too ruined to be habitable. We began noticing activity away from the approach trenches, diggings that puzzled us until someone untangled the clues: contagion was among the besiegers and they were burying their dead. Confirmation of an outbreak came soon enough when the enemy began catapulting corrupt bodies over our walls, intending to pollute both our air and our will to fight but our fighting strength started to grow and we simply burned the corpses.

On St Andrew's Day in February 1344, a sizeable fleet sailed in, a flotilla so large there was not room enough in the harbour and you could have walked from deck to moored deck across it. A flood of men-at-arms poured onto the quays and the billeting officers were beside themselves to find places for men to sleep. Eventually, some of the newcomers slept and ate aboard their ships, others took over homes, churches and public buildings while the cooks and provender suppliers set up outdoor kitchens and storage places.

I was delighted to find that a contingent of Cheshire and Welsh archers under the command of a Gwent mercenary called Robert

Roberts had joined the diverted crusade, for such longbowmen would be a valuable asset in battle. Rob Knollys assigned me and the handful of other English archers to them and, later, that probably saved my life.

The Mongols could see how crowded with shipping was our harbour but, and I never understood why, they made no move to attack it and they did not seem to realise that the reinforcements were as great a force as they were. Certainly, they tried to tempt us out from behind our solid walls. From time to time, they'd capture a Christian sentry or spy or messenger. They would bring the hapless individual up close to our walls but remain out of bowshot. Then they'd torture him, sometimes flaying him alive and cutting out his stomach; sometimes parading him around, blindfolded and helpless in shackles while he was stabbed with spears and beaten with horsewhips before being hanged from a convenient tree.

The poor wretches' screams and pleas for mercy could easily be heard and so inflamed our soldiers that several times some attempted a rescue, only to be captured themselves and subjected to similar tortures. For a week after Christian's disappearance, I waited in trepidation to see if he would be tormented in such a way but he was never evident, and we assumed he had been killed or maybe taken as a slave during the skirmish. What we could not even imagine was that the boy would one day bring freedom to most of England.

Before that distant day, we had to deal with the Golden Horde. Their actions caused a huge upwelling of hatred for the cruel Tatars and our men-at-arms were eager for battle when the Genoese commander Sanpietro ordered us to prepare for an attack at dawn the next day. He divided our forces that night, after we had confessed our sins, been shriven, and given absolution. Sanpietro sent galleys laden with soldiers plus our contingent of English archers and a strong force of

Genoese arbalesters out around a small headland to the west. There, we disembarked under a quarter moon onto a shingle beach and, under strict orders to wrap and muffle our weapons and make no noise on pain of flogging, followed guides three miles steeply inland on sheep tracks through the juniper brush. We emerged in the pre-dawn gloom behind the Turkic lines. Apart from a handful of scouts a few hundred yards in advance, we longbowmen led the long column of invaders.

Just after we had crested a rise and seen the gleam of the sea ahead, the archer Robert Roberts hissed, 'Down, boys, down!' and we sank gratefully into the thigh-high brush to rest and ready ourselves. A score or so of Georgian cavalry, expert in handling horses, slipped away from our force under orders to infiltrate the Mongol horse lines and, at a signal, to release the beasts. Another small group of scouts also went on ahead into the dark, armed with tinderboxes and candles to use for signalling. Their task was to locate the enemy, silence any outlying sentries and to bring us forward when the way was clear. All we now had to do was wait until we were unleashed like war dogs.

The sun rose behind us, useful as it would conceal us somewhat from watchers and we observed as the Mongols' camp stirred into life. Cookfires smoked, men strolled to latrines, sentries were changed and a growing bustle began. Lines of men formed to collect hot food; all was ordinary and quiet, until matters erupted. A flood of soldiers spilled out from the sally ports of Caffa, spreading silent like water and moving briskly towards the Mongol lines, where drums began beating and men were scrambling to grab weapons and armour.

I saw dark lines flickering towards the besiegers and realised they were showers of arbalesters' bolts; then men began falling and we could hear thin screams floating up to where we watched. Word came to us: 'Up, boys, quietly.' We rose from the brushy slopes and began

78

half trotting down the winding sheep paths towards the conflict we could see growing beneath us. Scouts crouching in the brush made urgent signals to move us to the right and I found they had directed us to a sheep-nibbled area of turf that overlooked the growing battle. Quiet-pitched orders came to us: 'Archers, here and here.' Captains were shunting us into position but there was still no response from the Mongols now just a couple of hundred paces away, downslope. Another quiet order: 'Plant your shafts!' It made sense. We began sticking arrows point first into the turf ahead of our stands. When we began firing, we'd reload faster by plucking an arrow from the turf than by fumbling for it in a quiver and we wanted the surprise and the storm of arrows to be as complete, shocking and deadly as it could be. And it was.

While we archers and arbalesters set up, the men-at-arms had trotted by, as stealthy as a she-fox approaching a henhouse. They poured down the slope and spread like water across our front, a hundred or so paces ahead of us. They had almost formed their ranks when the Mongols spotted them and began yelling. Our captains at once gave us the signal to fire – an upward pump of a fist that triggered us to elevate our longbows and begin releasing steel-tipped ash high into the air, one clothyard missile every six seconds. The flight took about nine seconds so we had each released two arrows and were notching a third before the first flights hammered down on men's necks and backs. As their comrades screamed and fell, the Mongols turned to look and dozens of them took arrows full in the face. Inwardly, I squirmed for them. I'd seen men who took an arrow in the head or face, and they almost never survived.

But, in the disciplined rhythm of pluck, notch, draw and release, an archer has little time to do anything else or even to think; once or twice, over the twang and whistle of the released arrow and its passage through the air, I discerned the clank and whoosh as our arbalesters stepped into the stirrup of their weapons, cranked their cables taut and triggered their heavy quarrels, once every thirty or so heartbeats. Their rate of fire was five times slower than that of a longbow but they had some advantages, chiefly that of the years of training needed to produce a skilled archer.

Rob Knollys was at my elbow, shouting encouragement. I did not break my rhythm and hardly spoke: I was grunting with the effort of pulling the weight of a man every time I drew the bowstring to my ear. 'You're crushing those fellows!' Rob, a fighting man but no archer, shouted. I paused after the next release to see the results of our attack and was gratified to see a tideline of sprawled bodies where our arrow-storm was still lashing down. I notched my next shaft and was on the point of releasing it when our captains began shouting at us to cease firing. Our companions who had sallied from the city were almost among the Mongols and were storming into their disarrayed formation.

As the besiegers fought, the Christian men-at-arms in front of us ran into the melée and began hacking and stabbing at the backs of the Mongols who were facing the other way, to repel the attack. In minutes, they broke and ran, stamping hundreds of their own under their armoured feet when a third force of mounted knights poured out of Caffa and crashed into their flank. At about the same moment, the Mongols' own horse herd stampeded through the running men, a throng of frantic animals released and panicked by our squad of Georgian horsemen. A few Mongols somehow scrambled onto the terrorised mounts, but they were mostly weaponless and simply fled. The hapless infantry was ridden down by the Christians and those that formed several desperate fighting stands were shot flat by our arrows and bolts.

The chroniclers later said that 15,000 Turks, Tatars and Mongols died that day. I know that many were executed by vindictive Christians after they were overwhelmed and disarmed. The mud of the killing field was slimed red with blood; the carrion crows feasted for days and the crusaders set cowed prisoners to digging grave pits and covering with quicklime the corpses thrown into them. But plague followed anyway. *Deus Vult* – God must indeed have wished it.

Chapter 11

Flea

Fang Guozhen gazed pensively across the churning waters of the South China Sea, admiring the wooded hills, well-watered orchards and tea gardens and the bright green rice paddies in their ordered terraces on the gentle lower slopes of his home province. He knew well this Luzon strait between the humped mainland and the rolling western plains of the island Liuqiu, for he had been sailing there since childhood. His family were shipowners and traders but, when just a boy, he had been taken as a slave by the Golden Horde of Turkic horsemen who had swept out of the Steppes and crushed the Chinese.

Guozhen had done well, had risen to be a trusted servant of a Tatar khan called Erdene. When the khan died of plague, Guozhen had quietly returned to China but an altercation in a tavern left a man dead and the former slave fleeing the mainland for his clan's holdings in the islands. Fortune smiled on him; he had used their family wealth and his three brothers' cunning and contacts and in time built a powerful fleet that taxed anything that sailed along this coastline.

His trading fleet had long practiced a sideline of piracy and the officials of the Yuan lords were on his payroll so turned a blind eye to the activity, especially since he had been transporting grain to the Yuan capital, Dadu for the warlord Zhang Shicheng, and had sent a son to another commander, Zhu Yuanzhang as a hostage. Now he was considering if it was yet time to turn away from piracy, to offer his fleet to the Yuan secretariat, be pardoned and to live at court as an honoured noble.

But there was a cloud on the horizon. A captain who had visited the khanate at Shandong had returned from the mighty Yellow River two days before with his cargo of textiles and grain undelivered, to report there was a Jurchen rebellion causing much trouble. The clan resented having to supply their Mongol masters with gyrfalcons; the place was in turmoil and warehouses had been looted and fired. The captain had been advised at the dock to stay aboard and mount guards over his cargo and to keep strangers off his ship. He understood the warning and had turned back for home before his ship was pillaged by rioters.

Almost as an afterthought, the captain added there was also a pestilence wracking the land, made worse because the Yellow River was in severe flood and people were trapped and unable to flee the plague.

Physicians said the contagion was carried by traders and even by ships' rats. However it came, it was a fury of fast-moving fevers. Most victims died within three or four days of their first symptoms; some went to bed healthy and happy and died in agony before morning. Physicians who went to treat the sick sometimes died even before their patients did.

The victim's nervous system collapsed and bizarre disorders made the hapless sufferer perform a staggering 'dance of death'. In just a matter of hours, the doomed sank into frenzied, raving madness and died in evident great pain.

The plague struck and killed with terrible speed. Many were well at the noon meal but were dead by suppertime. Terrified parents abandoned their sickened children; tradesmen refused to visit a home they suspected of infection and only the religious orders were left to tend to the sick and dying. The honest monks saw it as their duty to give the victims a proper burial and a hope of salvation in the afterlife but they paid a terrible price for their devotion. Soon, each monastery was emptied and echoing, the brothers themselves dead of the pestilence.

Fang Guozhen had listened to the incoming shipmaster, heard impassively of the horrors raging up the coast and mentally moved on. Next, he pondered decisions about moving the cargo he had in his warehouse. As he leaned on the rail, an insect bit the nape of his neck. He slapped at it with his hand and looked at his palm. No blood, not a mosquito, then. Maybe it was a flea whose carapace had protected it. Despite what he had heard of the contagion, he made no connection, gave the matter of an insect bite no more thought and went back to his internal debate, drumming his long fingernails on the rail. Would giving the emperor his fleet buy him favour? Probably, but when to make the gift? He'd sleep on it. As for the cargoes unexpectedly back in his warehouse, he could sell the grain in Liuqiu. It would not get the best price but there would be no huge loss. The textiles were more of a problem, for the local market had more than enough. Maybe he could send them overland by camel train along the trade routes called the Silk Road. The Venetians and Genoese would trade gold and wool for them. That might be a good solution.

Somewhere in the hold of Fang's high-sterned sailing vessel, a rat that had brought fleas aboard scratched a nest in a pile of old sacking.

An arm's length away, cosy in a roll of Yuan textiles, other fleas were laying eggs. They looked like small grains of white rice and would not be noticed by the labourers who moved the fabric to the camel train that would soon embark on the Silk Road.

Chapter 12

Genoa

Robert Roberts, the Gwent mercenary who headed a contingent of Welsh and English archers, spat over the side of the galley as we sailed through the narrows of the Bosporus. He jerked a thumb at the land to our left. 'Not sorry to be leaving that place,' he said, 'lot of heathens and the food's terrible.'

'Want ham, do you?' I joked.

'That would be splendid,' he said, 'but those poor benighted Muslims don't know good stuff when they see it. Now, a bit of Welsh mutton would be even better.' He sighed, wistfully.

'You'll soon be scoffing that,' I said. 'We'll be in Venice in a few more days and we could be in England in ten more.'

Roberts and I were standing at the stern of the Saint Matthew, a Genoese trading galley. On our left were the spires and mina-rets of Asian Constantinople; on our right, masons were putting finishing touches to the Galata Tower that stood as the last outpost on the continent of Europe. We'd defended Caffa, a Genoese trading site on the Black Sea, slaughtering more than ten thousand of the

Mongols' Golden Horde that had sought to sack the city. Now, we were going home.

The journey was smooth, the weather good and we sailed into Genoa happy to pay tribute at the cathedral of San Lorenzo for our safe travels. Afterwards, I strolled alone between the wharves, magnificent buildings and fine churches, admiring the energy and wealth of the city. I was considering how matters had changed in my life. In such a short time, I had gone from serfdom as a worker of the land, to crusader and neo-soldier thanks to my time with the Folville gang and, more importantly, to Robert Knollys' weapons training and advice. I'd fought in a siege, sailed on warm seas, seen a Pope and visited exotic cities. As I mused, I paid little attention to my surroundings and blundered into two youths as I turned a corner.

I stumbled backwards but one of the young men fell to the ground. His companion hissed at me and began to pick him up. I started forward to help and they both swore at me. My long-ago training with the monks had given me some simple Latin. The youths were Italian; the language was half-comprehensible and their anger was obvious.

'Scusi,' was all I could say in the confusion, taking in their velvet caps and expensive, colourful clothing. These were no peasants; they seemed to be young aristocrats. Certainly, they were quick-tempered, for although I gestured a half-apology, the one who had fallen swore at me again and pulled a dagger from his belt. I fumbled out my own knife as the second youth also produced a dagger and slashed at me rapidly, gashing my forearm with two parallel cuts. As I clutched at the wound, my knifepoint caught in fabric and clattered to the stones. At once, one of them kicked it away and the youths began to circle me, weapons at the ready, looking to step in and knife me. All I could do was to flee. I leaped forward, straight-armed one of them into the wall and ran for my life. They followed, shouting.

A handsome stone square bordered with gardens and fine houses opened up and I ran diagonally across it, aware that the noise of my pursuers was growing closer. Ahead of me was a taverna with a couple of tables and benches outside and I made for it, hoping to get inside before my pursuers could catch me. I arrived only five or so paces ahead of them, skidded around a wooden table and spotted a broom leaning against the wall. In a second, I had it in my hand as an improvised quarterstaff. My first lucky swipe knocked one youth's dagger aside and I retreated to put my back to a wall.

My attackers split up and approached from either side and I knew I would soon be a dead man. That was when San Lorenzo sent me a miracle. A familiar Welsh voice sounded. Robert Roberts and two of his archers had been inside the tavern and heard the commotion. Behind them was the innkeeper, armed with a cudgel. 'Now then, boys, put those knives away,' said Robert. His meaning was clear even if his language was not and he produced a wicked-looking poniard to support his request. My pursuers stepped back a pace and the shorter of the two began a rush of words.

The innkeeper, eager not to have blood spilled on his premises, interpreted. 'You have insulted one of the Doria clan, signore,' he told me. 'They are very important in Genoa.'

'It was an accident, and they stabbed ME!' I retorted, showing my slashed arm.

There was some rapid-fire conversation between the innkeeper and the youths; the tough-looking Welsh archers crowded closer and my attackers sullenly put their daggers away.

'Best put your broom down, Tom,' said Robert, 'or the master here will have you sweeping the whole place.'

'You'll also need an apron,' said one of his archers, 'if you're serving ale as well.'

'Let's get that cut seen to,' said Robert, tugging me into the gloom of the tavern. 'That'll make an interesting scar.' It did, and it later identified me when I did not want to be known.

But that was in the future. The matter with the Dorias was settled. They offered to pay a physician to tend my arm and, in return, I promised not to bring charges for my wounding. We left Genoa within the week.

Robert and I and five of his archers crossed the Alps on horseback, came to the Rhine River at Basel and were transported swiftly and smoothly downriver to the North Sea at Amsterdam, where we caught a cog to carry us to Kent. There, I took a room in a tavern in Canterbury, reasoning that the city was so thronged with pilgrims I'd be reasonably anonymous in case the hue and cry over my killing of Ottercombe was not forgotten.

On balance, I was doing well. I had a good store of gold plundered from the Mongols and King Edward helped, too. He had recently issued three new gold coins: a florin, a leopard and a helm, but his mint had put more gold into each than the coin's face value justified. A friendly goldsmith alerted me to the error and I traded Mongol gold for Edward's coins at a small discount and greatly improved my wealth when a coiner took my English money and converted it into new gold pieces. The royal mint withdrew the generous shillings before that summer was ended but my goldsmith friend and I were well satisfied.

Now no longer a villein but a reasonably wealthy man, I pondered my future. I could be a soldier: I'd enjoyed my military experiences at the siege and, still in my early twenties, I was young and hardy enough. I could be a tradesman, thatching houses, but that held little appeal. Trading was not for me; I was no merchant and I did not want to go back to working as a semi-slave to grow crops for some manorial lord. I'd rather be anything: even a chantry singing-clerk who couldn't sing. The thought made me laugh aloud and my mood lightened.

My path became clear as I strolled through the butter market just outside the cathedral precincts. A dark-haired man of my own age, in clothes that said he was a working man, was standing on an upturned tub to address a small crowd. He was criticising the landowners and the church itself, asking why we peasants had to support idle nobles and fat churchmen? He repeatedly spoke a small couplet, waving his arms for tempo to conduct his audience with: 'When Adam delved and Eve span, who was then the gentleman?' It was repeated often enough that the crowd began delightedly chanting it with him and I wondered how long it would be before the archbishop's tipstaffs got word and retainers came to disperse the mob. Then I wondered why they should; who was in the wrong? Were the common people wrong to protest at their misuse? Were the nobility in the right when they trod us down? It seemed a conflict was coming and I felt I should join in. My next thought was: if there is strife, should I learn to fight?

I listened until I heard the bell for Nones, remembered I had things to do and hurried away. At last, I remembered where I'd seen the young man before. He was from Ashlea, a village near Bowerfield and he'd been at a gathering in our village tavern when a north country man had said we should organise against our masters. That day, the young speaker stood up to say it should be done, and soon. The monks' greed had caused his baby sister to starve and die; they had taken the family's small store of money and some of their crops as a tithe, leaving them with nothing. And nothing was what had happened and nothing looked even likely to be done to right that wrong. What was his name? 'Wat!' I said as memory flooded in. He'd said, 'Walter – call me Wat.' I thought I should seek him out. Maybe my villager friends' lives could be improved. It would be good to try, anyway, for I had little sympathy with greedy churchmen and even greedier lords of the manor. I resolved to visit Master Walter and talk to him about teaching these arrogant masters a lesson.

Chapter 13

Plotters

Wat the tiler and his father were roof tile makers, not conspirators, and they knew what was right and just. They knew that Christ did not teach that we should burden the poor or treat our fellow man like field beasts. They had suffered injustice but had nowhere to turn to get redress. The church insisted on its tithes under pain of losing your immortal soul and even the lord of the manor had no legal power over the clergy. That was why, at the king's wishes, Thomas Becket had been murdered: because he refused to give up the practice of the church judging its own clergy's failings.

King Henry had been cowed into walking barefoot to do penance at Canterbury for Becket's death and ninety monks whipped his back as he passed. Wat knew the tale and knew too that if churchmen could so humble a king, what chance did a commoner have of gaining justice from the clergy?

'There is no hope of a bishop ruling against one of his ordained own,' said Wat the tiler as we sat outside his small cottage near Maidstone. 'We cannot force them to do anything.'

'But we can!' interjected Owen Blackburn, the leech gatherer, who was still quietly mustering support around the area. I'd invited him along in the half-hope that we could begin some cooperative movement that would improve the peasants' lot and, maybe, our own.

Blackburn leaned forward eagerly. 'If we band together, we can do much,' he insisted. 'We can make the monks take less from us if we all refuse to supply them except on our terms. If we stick together, we can reduce the number of days we have to work for no reward – those in the manors will have no choice if we all stop working for free. They'll starve if they have to grow their own grain. We can even get the king's collectors to reduce taxes. The king wants our silver to pay for his wars; well, if we won't hand it over and if we stay united, there are too many of us for them to forcibly collect and so the king will just have to stop going to war, or he'll have to find some other way to pay for it.'

The prospect of peace, lower taxes and more rewards for our labours was heady and we looked at each other questioningly. 'We could even be allowed to live where we wanted, not be chained to the manor's lands,' said Wat. 'If men could seek work anywhere, they could get a fair wage for their work. The masters would know we could move on if they don't pay, and the crops won't gather themselves. They've even imported foreigners who take the gold out of our country and leave useless luxuries in exchange. The outsiders also take the best jobs while our own workers starve.'

Owen nodded. 'That's right. East Anglia is full of Zeelanders and Flemings that the king brought in and they control the wool trade. We have hundreds of apprentices to mercers, tanners, bakers and the like who've served their time but are not allowed to become masters, because the aldermen want to keep them as mere hired workers who only get low pay.'

'We wouldn't have to pay all those damned taxes,' I said. 'No heriot death tax to be handed over; we could inherit our father's things without paying dues to a stranger. The collectors seize the best beast when a tenant dies; the church takes another for the tithes they assume he underpaid and we must face a tax when a daughter marries, or when we sell a horse or a cow – why should a rich lord take all that?'

Owen said thoughtfully: 'The mayor and aldermen don't care about us. They elect their own. They raise taxes and take on public debts but don't bother to consult the people whose sweat pays for it all.' It was true: the wealthy kept wages low, the aldermen fined people who refused to work and they all tried to dissolve the guilds that journeymen formed in hopes of bettering their conditions. He looked steadily at us and added quietly: 'We have to make a fraternity that can stay together and we have to do it quietly or they'll break it apart and nothing will improve.' Privately, I thought we might need to use force to get our way and I resolved to improve the military skills I'd learned at Caffa.

Then, a chilling thought struck me. If we went against church and king, we would lose, unless we could force them both to back down. And how, Tom, I asked myself, would that happen? The answer was blindingly obvious. If we grumbled and made powerless threats, our ringleaders would be hanged, or worse, we'd be cowed into submission for a generation. We had to bargain from a position of strength. And the strength in England was assumed to be the armoured knights who slew hapless peasants on the battlefield.

We peasants had to be as strong as those fighting men. We needed to make a peasant army, to train and equip them and show the fighting knights we could overwhelm them. Only then would we be free from their boots on our necks. We had to forge an uprising and convince the commons to prepare them to go to war, scythes and pitchforks against lances and swords. But we also had something else.

We had archers. Every man of age was dutied by law to train as an archer. It was a training that took years but the resulting fighting man terrified England's enemies and the archers alone could be enough to make England's armoured, mounted lords reconsider their villeins and serfs. We'd shown that at Crecy and Poitiers. The longbowmen in battle had slaughtered England's enemies and they could do it again, to whomever. That very threat could bring an agreement with King Edward's men.

That was why we began to create our secret societies. There was no overall structure, just village after village of discontented people, a seething, muttering population waiting for a spark to ignite an uprising. And matters got worse before they were better.

In early 1345 a great comet moved across the sky; an omen, men said, of terrible things to come. Almost at once came news of a massacre of crusaders by the Turks under Umar Beg; England was at war after our king, who banned the use of the French language at court, declaring: 'We are Englishmen. We need no foreign tongue here!' offered open defiance to Philip of France, who claimed to be his overlord. We entered another expensive war. The weather worsened; we had snow at Easter and all the signs were that the crops would fail. It would be a starvation year.

On a late spring day, I went into Rochester for the market and came across a remarkable sight: a pair of pageant wagons. These were high-sided, roofed wagons which acted as mobile theatres. They were dragged through the streets from station to station and then parked in an open place as a temporary stage. One was viewed end-on and the other opened its side so the crowd could watch the actors and chorus as they performed.

The usual plays, like the one I was watching outside the cathedral, had a religious theme. My entertainment that day was called 'Mary Magdalene Washing Christ's Feet' and it was presented by members of the Weavers' Guild. Placards announced to those who could read that the other wagon, which was shrouded and quiet, would present 'The Marriage Feast of Cana' when the bell rang for Vespers. Its cast was drawn from the company of Shearmen and Taylors.

I stood among the crowd enjoying the Magdalene play and a young fellow who was one of the actors pushed through with a collecting bowl. I dropped in more than I meant, a whole silver penny, and he thanked me effusively. Something in his voice sent a note through my brain and I asked him where did he live?

'Well, master,' he said, 'I live everywhere and nowhere because I travel with my company, but I was born not far from here, in Deal.'

A Kentish man. 'You travel?'

He smiled proudly. 'Been everywhere, Lincoln, York, Oxford,' he said.

'And how are you received?'

'Some people envy me, some disparage me as a mere playactor. I don't care.'

'Who disparages you most?'

'That's easy. It's always the wealthy who say I should be working, although I don't see them getting their hands dirty.'

I wanted to know how others in England felt so I offered him a mazer of ale. He accepted and we talked in a nearby tavern. Yes, he felt the common folk were hard pressed and were resentful. Yes, he had heard of peasants forming cooperative groups – they were similar in many ways to the guilds like his own Scriveners' company that put on the morality plays. And the big question also got a yes: he was willing to spread a message around England, urging locals to form groups and present their grievances to their masters. 'If people hear that others are doing the same, we might effect change,' I urged. But matters delayed our forming associations of the common people.

Chapter 14

France

Bad weather meant failed crops. Many, unable to pay rents, had already
been put out of their homes, so starving peasants wandered abroad in
search of work and food. Somehow, I'd been found by four members
of my own Thatcher clan from Broadstairs, a town named for a flight
of steps to a shrine atop a chalk cliff. The four men, all but one of
them young, had come seeking me in my lodgings in Canterbury
because I was a kinsman rumoured to be wealthy. 'You could make us
a loan, Cousin Tom,' they said. 'We'll repay you next summer when
we get a crop.' The timing was providential: the previous day, a herald
outside the cathedral close had announced that the king's son, Prince
Edward of Woodstock, was recruiting archers and men-at-arms to
accompany him to the wars in France.

'You can earn money as a soldier,' I told them. 'The herald offered
archers three pence a day, plus boots, cloaks, the use of a horse and
all the plunder you can take. Men-at-arms get two pence a day. Be
a soldier for a year or two and come back a rich man.' I knew from
Robert Knollys, already a rising captain among the *routier* freebooter

companies, that a man could become wealthy in a short time at war. 'I'm thinking of going,' I announced. I wasn't inspired by the money, as I had a good stash of gold, but I was young and hot-headed, had enjoyed the fighting at the siege of Caffa and wanted to test my new skills. There was also the not-so-small matter of Ottercombe's death. I might still be recognised and dragged to jail or hanged. A year or two elsewhere might ensure my safety.

'Aye, I could go,' said the oldest of the group, a relative greybeard of thirty-six years. 'I fought at Dupplin Moor in '32 when we routed the Scots.'

'That would do, Joseph,' I said. 'Experienced soldiers are much in demand.'

The other cousins, Thatcher brothers named Edgar, Jude and Henry, assured me they practised diligently with the longbow and not just at the mandatory Sunday training sessions. I viewed their heavily muscled arms and shoulders, allowed that they were about as big as mine and opined that a recruiting serjeant would snap them up, too.

In a rush of bonhomie, we agreed to go together. We'd make our way to Dover to join the prince and his forces once we had made a few preparations. As they believed I was the wealthiest one, I assumed the role of leader. Joseph might have had the post but he was not an archer, was paid a penny a day less than the others and was in their eyes old and decrepit. I did not argue. So, we set off walking to Dover Castle, where we found the prince was embarking from the Solent. An obliging shipmaster who was taking supplies to the army allowed us aboard and we sailed west down-Channel, past the Isle of Wight, and into the great harbour at Portsmouth.

There, everything was crowded and bustling yet, somehow, among the throngs of strangers, I found myself staring at a familiar figure – Robert Knollys. He pushed his way through the crowd to hug me and slap my back. 'Good to see you, Tom,' he said. 'You're coming to whip the French, eh?' Rob seemed to know everything and was, I found out later, held in high regard as a soldier by both the young prince and his father, Edward of Windsor, King of England, Lord of Ireland and claimant to the French throne. He had raised an army of 12,000 men to underscore that claim and planned to make mounted raids across France, creating havoc and destruction to demonstrate how the current French king, John, was unable to protect his people. With John's standing weakened, Edward would step forward.

King Edward already had two small expeditionary forces operating on the continent: one in Flanders, the other in Gascony. He had intelligence that King John's army was away chasing Henry of Grosmont, the Duke of Lancaster, in Gascony and accelerated his plans. He assembled a fleet of seven hundred cogs and chose to make the longer sea crossing to Normandy, thereby avoiding the French warships which expected to intercept us on the short Dover-Calais sea route. Edward would then raid east to Paris, living off the land and ransacking as he went. With luck the *chevauchée* – mounted raid – would force John and his house of Valois from the throne and be a satisfying dish of cold revenge for the humiliating terms the arrogant French king had obliged Edward to agree to early in his reign.

Edward also wanted his sixteen-year-old son Edward of Woodstock to learn the art of war and, on a July day when we landed in France at a place called St Vaast, he knighted the prince in a square-towered local church and gave him the prestigious command of the vanguard of the army. The young Edward looked the part: tall, swarthy, black-moustached even as a youth and with an imperious air worthy of his title of Prince of Wales.

He had advice from the Earls of Warwick and Northampton, seasoned warriors both, but confidently issued clear and exact instructions of his own: the horsemen should equip themselves with shield, lance, sword, dagger, longbow and arrows. In the train of the mounted men would follow pack animals carrying supplies and equipment like axes, augers, boards and spades. There would be some food, clothing and arms carried as spares, but based on the planning of Robert Knollys and others like him who had gone ahead, the prince had arranged supply dumps along his planned route. This reduced the slow-moving impedimenta carts and allowed fast travel and lightning attacks. He also kept wagons to a minimum, instead using sumpter beasts from a herd of 6,000 riding and pack horses, almost all of them shipped from England.

'The king's purpose,' explained Knollys, 'is not to besiege well-fortified towns; it's to create havoc across large swathes of land and wreck the people's confidence in their monarch. It's "strike hard, strike fast and move on" before the enemy can organise resistance. Edward's also being strict about taking prisoners. They're a nuisance if you capture them early in a conflict – you have to control and guard them, which takes you away from the fighting. They can be profit-able: ransoms of money or land for a wealthy prisoner can be huge and there's always a knight's expensive armour to be taken as booty, but a foot soldier with no more than a few coins in his pocket: well, it's easier just to kill him. Edward wants only wealthy prisoners kept alive, chained until battle's end and under minimal guard.'

I'd not had proper armour during the siege at Caffa, so I asked Rob, who was an experienced soldier, to explain the alternatives. 'Your harness?' he said. 'There are two dozen pieces in a body harness that uses plate. They start with sabatons to cover your feet and go all the way to a steel "comb" which strengthens the helm over your head. Some parts are hinged, like the poleyns over the knees and the vambraces at the elbows and a gorget for neck and throat. You wear the elements over a padded tunic or a lanolin-greased leather jerkin which allows the metal to move freely.'

'For myself,' said Rob, 'I do not like to fight wearing a closed helmet that obscures my vision and a lot of soldiers prefer, as I do, a thigh-length shirt of flexible chain mail – linked rings – because it's lighter and easier to move in.' I took Rob's advice and chose to wear a bascinet helmet, open-faced to allow lateral vision and with a tail that gave good protection for the neck; a mail shirt was also what I settled for and it served me well. I noticed some brighter patches of new links where the mail had been repaired and assumed some unfortunate had been speared or stabbed while wearing it so I scrubbed it all with fine sand and made the whole thing uniformly bright.

When we arrived in Normandy, most of our fleet could not berth in the snug harbour of St Vaast, so we landed the bulk of our men, horses and equipment on a sandy beach nearby and at dawn the next day began our march inland. A detachment scoured the coastal towns and captured one hundred or more trading ships while the bulk of the army looted and burned the unguarded hinterland, sending back booty on the captured vessels to be ferried to England.

After a fortnight's havoc, we came to the town of Caen where the walled old city had a formidable castle augmented by two stout stone abbeys but the new town depended mostly on the barrier of the River Orne and several fortified bridges for its defences. King Edward rode into our camp with a troop of knights and waved his captains into a pavilion. I slid in behind Knollys, eager to see the king up close. Edward wasted no time on preliminaries.

'The French have made a mistake. I expected we'd need to besiege this place and we are not equipped for that but the burghers pressured the garrison commander into defending the new town where their homes and warehouses are; they've abandoned their strongest defences – the castle and walled old town – to hide behind some scratched-together timber ramparts.' He scanned the pavilion and its crowd of sombre faces. 'We'll take the bridges and the new town, then assault the castle where the walls are crumbling. An escalade should succeed; there are only several hundred of the garrison in there, although there are more than a thousand men-at-arms but not many archers in the new town.'

Our first target, the two abbeys which we thought would be strong redoubts, proved to hold a surprise: they had been abandoned. The prince was readying to attack the fortified bridges when a body of Welsh archers, flushed with wine, booty and two weeks of easy victories, acted first. Eager to loot the town, they made a mad rush at the fortified bridges. The Earl of Warwick tried to control his half-drunken men but was too late. The die was cast – and it rolled a six.

Several hundred Welsh archers had battled their way across two of the bridges when the garrison commander made a fatal mistake. He sent most of his command and about three hundred armed citizens outside the safety of their walls to contest the crossing. A horde of English and Welsh men-at-arms waiting to advance across the bridges discovered that the tidal river was running low and was easily fordable. Soon, they were wading across, longbows and quivers held dry above their heads and they established themselves on the far bank. Their blizzard of arrows cleared the battlement's fighting platforms above their heads and a troop of Cumberland spearmen swarmed over and through the gates; the Black Boars, as the French called English soldiers, were inside the city.

For five days, murder, rape and pillage followed, only to end when fire began to consume the once-fine buildings. Every street corner had its pile of heaped loot, from kitchen wares to tapestries; church vestments were scattered about, their small jewels ripped from them, and small huddles of soldiers could be seen hacking to pieces silver and gold patens, chalices, pyxes and other church treasures to divide them up and to make them unidentifiable should any superior take unkindly to stealing from a church.

Everywhere, bodies lay in the streets among scattered household goods and, here and there, some unfortunate was being tortured to reveal the hiding place of his small treasures. I saw one grey-bearded Jew hung upside down above a small fire, another with his hands being smashed. 'He's a pagan moneylender,' explained a soldier who was watching. 'He leeches off honest people. We're just getting their money back.'

Even the king had no mercy and sent horsemen out to cut down refugees who had tried to escape the carnage. 'He wants to make an example of them. They resisted his demand to surrender,' said Rob grimly. 'Others in the next towns we invest will remember – and open the gates.' I made a point of wearing my mail shirt and carrying at least a long knife and my stout quarterstaff wherever I went. Too many drunken soldiers might decide to see if I had any loot on me that they wanted.

My kinsmen Joseph, Jude, Edgar and Henry made a point of staying together – even Englishmen were not safe from drunken fellow Black Boars. 'We never thought matters would be this bad,' said Joseph, the eldest of them. 'There is no charity here.'

I repeated what Rob Knollys had said was the king's reasoning: to make an example of those who resisted him.

'It's not the Christian way,' said Jude. I had to agree. It was war and half of Caen's population – 5,000 souls – died that July.

Our king was unmoved. He called his court together to pay their respects to his ancestor, Duke William of Normandy, at the royal burial place in Caen's abbey of St Etienne, then went on to pillage a half dozen other monasteries, dozens of farmhouses and a score of villages. Wherever we went, smoke rose. In time we were not its cause: the locals, under orders from their king, were scorching the earth, burning their crops and driving away their beasts to deny us the ability to live off the land. And all the time, a French army six or seven times our size was coming for us.

In camp that night, Rob Knollys had news: 'Duke John of Normandy is coming from the south with an army that will join John's force at Rouen. We must cross the Seine so we can retreat into Flanders but the bridges around Rouen have been destroyed to trap us. Prince Edward says we'll have to move fast to find a crossing.'

We did and for a week we raced north with the French in pursuit, travelling across a vast plain between the mighty Seine and the tidal Somme rivers. Ahead of us was the English Channel where all the ports were guarded; less than a couple of hours' march behind us was the huge French army. King John's scorched-earth policy meant our men and beasts were starving. We were weak and trapped. We had somehow to cross the Somme or die. And St George sent us his miracle.

At a place called Blanchetaque we found cart tracks that went down to the Somme and emerged on the other side, but the river was racing and plainly impassable. A peasant bribed with gold told us the secret: twice a day at low tide, a natural weir, a hard ridge of limestone about ten paces wide, came close to the water's surface and for a brief period could be used as a ford. The peasant told us the river then would come up to the chin of a small man. At dusk, we floated men across on wine tuns and set guide ropes across the river; in the middle of the night, at the lowest ebb of the tide we slipped all 12,000 of our men across despite resistance from a body of French arbalesters on the far bank.

We abandoned our wagons of booty but we found some forage for the animals and food for us. We then marched a short distance until, at a village called Crecy-en-Ponthieu, we found a place to make our stand. Edward chose to fortify some high ground, up whose constricted slope the enemy must advance. Our right flank was protected in part by the River Maye and by Crecy village itself which we defended; our left flank was secured by the also-defended village of Wadicourt and our rear by a forest some ten miles long and four miles deep: impossible terrain for cavalry. Edward sited the centre of our line behind a series of vineyard terraces and trenches designed to compress the advancing enemy even more.

He ordered pits dug in front of us in a chequerboard pattern and planted them with sharpened stakes, then scattered spiked caltrops to cripple any enemy cavalry that broke through. The king ordered almost all of the army to fight on foot, in three battles arrayed in a sawtooth pattern. Two were forward, the third battle and a cavalry force were held in reserve to the rear. The centre, forward battle was commanded by Prince Edward. To attack him and his tempting royal standard, the French must pass through a choke point that would be made worse by our archers firing into them and heaping up the wounded and dying. Those longbowmen were arrayed in a staggered line so men-at-arms could step through their ranks for hand-to-hand combat should the French break through. We also had nine 12-barrelled volley guns mounted on carts and interspersed along our front. They used gunpowder and fired twelve iron balls at a time, doing damage but also creating smoke, noise and confusion among the enemy horses.

A full twenty-four hours after we arrived at Crecy, the French came in a colourful horde, not in disciplined columns. Their best force, of 6,000 Genoese crossbowmen, professional mercenaries like those who had fought side by side with us at Caffa, plodded forward looking dusty and exhausted. They had marched fast in full harness, carrying their heavy weapons but had not brought the pavises that would shield them from our clothyard arrows. They were surrounded by a swirl of armed citizens who had come in search of plunder, and they were pushing and urging the soldiers forward in a weary, footsore mob.

A large body of French knights spurred through them, breaking what semblance of order there had been and many of the Genoese raised their arbalests and fired, almost randomly as if they wanted to discharge and leave. The shower of bolts fell well short. Rain an hour or so earlier had slackened their cables and left their crossbows near-useless. A shouted order and our longbowmen nocked, drew, marked and loosed 2,000 flickering shafts that darkened the sky as they hissed through it. Before the first blizzard of iron, birch and beech slammed into the enemy, another was in the air and a third was being loosed.

Our bodkin points smashed through armour, flesh and bone; the cannon boomed their unfamiliar, frightening sound and the screams of the wounded French overtopped all. Just a few knights made it through the pits, stakes and obstacles that included thrashing, screaming horses spiked through their hoofs by the deadly caltrops, but our pikemen stepped through the archers' ranks and dispatched the unseated, helpless knights as they struggled to rise in their heavy armour.

As the main body of John's nobles advanced, our archers kept up a merciless sleet, their shafts replenished by boys who ran to deliver linen bags full of sheaves of fresh arrows, and the leading edges – they were not ranks – of the enemy flinched and shied away. Their faltering caused them to curve towards the constricted centre of the killing field where the dead were piling up in heaps and swathes. Then the French stalled, encumbered by obstacles alive, dead and inanimate. Knollys saw the moment and, with the Lancashire knight Thomas Holland, led a force of archers to run a hundred paces across the blood-soaked turf and thump volley after volley into the enemy flank from range so close our bodkin points could pierce two inches of oak wood.

The flower of French nobility died in those moments. King John himself took an arrow in the face; almost every knight in his retinue was wounded or killed and the French turned and ran. The battle was won, though we fought small conflicts even past Vespers and murdered the wounded on the field by moonlight. Many of us, weary beyond belief, slept on the bloodied turf and woke in the morning mist to collect more than 2,000 proud heraldic banners that would never again announce their dead lords. The chroniclers said that 30,000 of King John's subjects ended their life's journey that day. For us, it opened the road to Calais and ships to England.

Chapter 15

Pestilence

The caravan of traders carried tea, porcelain, perfumes, dyes and silk from China to Europe along a network of tracks and caravanserai camps called the Silk Road that was travelled by missionaries, migrants, soldiers and refugees. They, unknowing, brought some death-dealing passengers travelling comfortably burrowed into rolls of fabric. Fleas, carrying foul disease.

The insects' journey began in China's Hebel province, where nine of every ten inhabitants died of the terrible plague the fleas carried.

Villages, towns, whole nations were ravaged as the pestilence spread almost before news of its coming could be conveyed. It took only a decade and a few hundred generations of fleas to spread like widening ripples in a pond until it covered the known world. Rats and marmots began it all, carrying the contagion in their bloodstreams across the widest Steppes, campaigning with the Golden Horde as it rampaged across Asia and infecting the animals' passenger fleas. They, in turn transmitted their fatal bites to humans and the pestilence spread from the Korea peninsula to China, where half the population perished.

The empty spaces of Turkistan might have proved a barrier to transmission but herdsmen on their seasonal migration to pasture their flocks transported the rodents and their insect riders and spread the affliction ever wider. In a few summer months, the plague bridged the geographical gap, wiping out three hundred tribes. Millions more died as the Black Death travelled the trade routes from one caravanserai to the next and then, rat-borne, sailed in ships' holds and fanned out across the sea.

From the Dark Lands and Celestial Mountains of central Asia, the Great Mortality entered India, the Caspian Sea, Syria, Armenia, Mesopotamia and the Mediterranean. Populations vanished; cities lost between four and seven of every ten citizens. So many there were not willing or able to bury the dead. The rotting corpses on town and village streets befouled the air and spread plague still further. The Mongol Empire collapsed after the outbreak devastated all four mighty khanates. The peace the Mongols had imposed had allowed trade across continents: the decision let the pestilence move freely. One in three Persians died and when the Mongols besieging Caffa for a second time added reinforcements from the east, they also brought the plague into their ranks. Before their leader Jani Beg gave up the siege after having lost four-fifths of his army to the pestilence, he ordered the corpses of his stricken troops to be catapulted over Caffa's walls, to discomfit the Italians within. It spread the outbreak even wider.

When those traders returned from the Black Sea to their warehouses in Venice and Genoa, they brought the contagion with them in their ships. The rats and fleas came ashore; the insects fed on human blood and half the population of the entire continent of Europe died in agony.

Chapter 16

Kent

Of the five Thatcher cousins, three of us left the king's army while it still besieged Calais, not tempted to stay by the prospect of booty. Two Thatchers opted to stay. Jude, the younger, liked the military life. He hoped to increase his fortune and he had no wife waiting in Kent. Edgar stayed, too. He probably wished he had no wife – his was a slatternly scold with a sharp tongue who had escaped the ducking stool by means I never understood. It was easy to see why he was not eager to go back to England. But we three had a fortune in our saddlebags as well as a missive for the banker Knights of the Temple in London's Fleet Street to cash. It was a heavy ransom for Bishop Coire of Dax, a fighting cleric whom we had captured at Crecy.

The oldest of us, Joseph wanted to return to Kent for his parents' sake. 'They are getting old and, with this booty, I can bring them comfort and ease in their last years. We can even do some good for ourselves and others of the clan,' he said. 'Perhaps we can get manumission – pay off the lord and rid ourselves of our feudal duties. He may sell to us, or we may find land of our own and be proper freemen.'

To this end, Jude and Edgar authorised us to use their share of the bishop's ransom and try to set up new lives for them against their return to England.

We all were in agreement. Like Henry, I had neither wife nor children but the prospect of working our own land as freemen was heady and we all discussed it eagerly. Joseph cautioned us, though: 'Do not reveal how much we acquired after the battle. We should agree a small amount and hold to that. Do not be boasting in the tavern. If the baron gets wind that we have serious gold, he will somehow rob us of it.' That made sense and all agreed, so we three returned to my cousins' village of Clisford, not to my own, for Baron Roger of Bowerfield would long remember I'd killed his man Ottercombe. We settled to a quiet life while Joseph began a prolonged bargaining with their baron. All seemed set for a good, new life when alarming news came.

Last week, eight people and a taverner in Dover had all died grossly and mysteriously quickly. A packman who came through Clisford took some delight in recounting the details and two or three of the wives happily relayed the news. What we would know as the Great Mortality was raging across southern Europe. Although we did not yet know it as such, Death was rapping at our door.

Its victims' first symptoms were uncontrolled sneezing, coughing, spitting of blood and heavy sweating. They reported feeling feeble, having aches and chills, acquired a white coating on the tongue and a black pustule where they had been flea bitten, often on the leg. Egg-sized boils, black and oozing blood, appeared in the groin and quickly spread to the armpits and neck. The victims' speech slurred; their balance was poor; they staggered and their skin took on red spots which went black, causing terrible pain.

Some unfortunates who were near the end of life began staggering, tormented, delirious and stumbling. Everything about them – breath, sweat, shit and piss – stank foully. A priest who had been summoned caught on his face droplets from his patient's sneezing and died more swiftly than his parishioners. The physician they'd called for was elsewhere and did not see the victims, so survived – for now. And the mortality spread faster than anyone would believe possible. Some said it was related to flea bites – victims who had been bitten saw black spots develop at the site. Some said their cats had eaten rats and passed the disease on to humans before dying themselves. Some blamed the Jews, who were cruelly persecuted. Others said it was God's retribution for our sins. We heard it all and shivered. We would not allow strangers into the village and we kept wary, ready to turn away even those we knew if we suspected their condition. We put coins and goods well outside the village boundaries in hopes that others, plague-free, would leave us food in exchange.

The local lord of the manor heard tales of depraved men who may have been infected or may have simply claimed to be so to get their way. They would threaten to enter homes and contaminate those within unless they were paid to leave with money, goods or sex. The baron appointed watchmen to guard against such outlaws and issued them with long pikes to keep the possibly infected blackmailers at a distance before they imprisoned them. Few watchmen stayed their rounds, for they were fearful of meeting a plague victim, although some were eager to guard the granary and storehouses because they could steal food there. Twice, a procession of bloodied flagellants passed through: groups of men who took it on themselves to end the pestilence by whipping their own backs. We watched from a distance, open-mouthed at their sacrifice, for they used knotted leather whips that carried small iron claws which turned their backs into pulped flesh.

Once, a sheriff's man rode in, eye-masked and with a vinegar-soaked leather piece over his mouth and nose. 'You must mark your doors with an 'X' if there is plague within,' he commanded. 'Bury the dead after nightfall in pits and cover them with quicklime. Burn all bedding and clothes of the pestilence victims and if one of you shows any signs of being infected but must tend his beasts or his crops, he is to avoid all contact with others. Physical contact causes death and so does breathing in the exhaled breath of an infected person.'

Some people used their last hours and fading strength to prepare for death, tying tags with their names onto themselves so others would know who they were when dead. Others simply prayed for safety and sought salvation from the few clergy prepared to care for the sick. Those clerics became an increasingly small number as the weeks went by and so many of them contracted the mortality that bishops authorised lay people to confess each other.

News came to us, uneasy news, news that made us wonder if we were fated; news of the deaths of entire populations of closed communities like jails, ghettos, castles, convents, monasteries and military camps: all places where people lived close to each other. They died *en masse*, together and suddenly. The rare travellers who passed by our village – men-at-arms returning home from France, a friar whose brethren had all died, a man driven mad with grief – kept a distance but shouted tales of silent settlements where all had died or fled. They told of bodies lying at roadsides or in fields, of lowing cattle trapped in their byres, complaining to be milked, of animals wandering through rotting, ungathered crops, unpicked orchards and untended gardens. They called out advice for protections against the pestilence: we should burn juniper or sage, bay or frankincense to cleanse the air in our homes. Religious medals were effective; a priest's blessing was helpful.

We could, they shouted, purify rooms by carrying burning herbs through them; we should heat flints in a fire then drop them into vinegar, an act which they said gave off purifying fumes. We must wash floors with a solution of mint, vinegar and pennyroyal and we should burn fires day and night to ward off the ill humours. Some said that butter was a good preventive and a broth of chamomile, powdered linseed, rose leaves and wheat would also aid our resistance to the disease, as would prayer and fasting. Some said a feather taken from the tail of a young pigeon would successfully pierce the buboes and draw out the evil humours; others claimed that splitting the bird from back to breast and laying it over the afflicted area would warm and draw out the deadly venom. None of it worked and we suffered and died.

A bold packman who continued his travels came by Clisford and told stories of congregations who had attended church services to pray for immunity from the malady but had died where they knelt together. In Italy, he'd heard mass graves were being dug in piazzas and colonnades because the graveyards were full; in France and Flanders, shrouded, putrid bodies lay in the streets, waiting for the death carts. Apothecaries wore bird-like masks, whose long beaks were stuffed with herbs and flowers to purify the air they breathed, but even those precautions and the voluminous clothes they wore as protection usually failed. A gallant monk in Spain had single-handedly cared for his twenty-eight fellow friars as they contracted the pestilence. He had given each the Last Rites and buried them in the monastery grounds, one after another, until he was all alone. Finally, the sole survivor of all his brothers, he too died.

Then the contagion came to England. The packman gave us the warning: 'The sheriff says the contagion came from France and went to Dorset and Bristol and Somerset. Now it's coming here.' We heard stories of parents who would not go near their sick children, of lawyers who refused to meet people who wanted wills made, of ships sailing into harbour with only one or two of the crew still alive. Relentlessly, the mortality spread.

In our county of Kent, hamlets and villages were emptying of the living and by autumn not even the fields were free of death. Pathetic wool bundles that were once sheep dotted the land; foetid, stinking bodies of swine, rabbits and rats littered the woods and downlands or rotted in hedges and ditches. Even the carrion crows would not touch those poisonous bundles. We kept to our own homes, prayed and mourned those we had buried. We fumigated, washed and scrubbed everything, scanned ourselves often, carefully seeking but not wishing to find any rash, blotch or blemish. We started nervously at every sneeze and cough and hoped, simply and fearfully, to survive. Despite our prayers and our actions, the pestilence spread like wildfire. Less than a twelvemonth after the first deaths in Somerset, there was no sanctuary from the plague anywhere in England; the king's sheriffs said that almost half of the population had died and that London, with its packed humanity and befouled rivers and streets, had suffered an even higher loss.

By Christmas, however, we had some small cause to celebrate: the number of deaths seemed to ease; the king had called a halt to the war with France and England owned the vital port of Calais. And, we had survived what men called the Great Mortality. Slowly and shakily, life resumed its normal course. After taking an oath to serve in the king's army if needed, I was released and returned to Bowerfield.

There, Baron Roger had taken his place in the churchyard and any thought of hunting me for Ottercombe's death was long forgotten.

For a small sum of gold that made the scarecrow priest's eyes gleam, I had Lizzie reburied inside the church itself. There she could rest until Gabriel blew his golden trumpet and she would more easily be carried up to heaven in the slipstreams of the saints. Next, I hung up my harness and weapons and began a time hopefully free of blood, smoke and death.

Chapter 17

Wool

The booty we Thatcher cousins had taken in France was greatly valuable in an England drained of wealth and shockingly emptied of population. We found that people wanted coin so they could independently move elsewhere and we could buy good properties, excellent beasts and good land for what was little more than a peppercorn. Joseph, Henry and I were joined by Jude, who came back from the siege of Calais as a tough, hardened longbowman. Edgar, victim of a Genoese arbalester's bolt, never returned and his scold of a wife had succumbed to the pestilence that devastated her village: just like hundreds of other villages which, if we could believe travellers' tales, were uninhabited, deserted and crumbling.

Joseph, as eldest, held our joint booty of coin, some small amount of jewellery and a sack full of chopped-up silver and gold that had once been church plate looted from places of worship across a swathe of France. He had exchanged the bishop's ransom note for coin at one of the Inns of Temple before the worst of the pestilence scoured London. 'We have gold and silver that the fat churchmen extorted from the faithful; they didn't deserve it anyway,' he told us as we met to make plans. 'Remember, there is no one person to say we are villeins anymore. Our manorial lords are dead; the parish priests who may have had records have gone, too, and there is no sheriff or serjeant who knows us or can say we have feudal duties any longer.'

So, we faced the question of what to do. None of us wanted to continue soldiering and we certainly no longer wished to be tied to a few strips of furrowed land. Joseph had a suggestion. 'England's wealth comes from wool,' he asserted. 'We used to send raw wool to Flanders to be made into cloth; then it was our own abbeys that took the wool, under long contracts that favoured them, only to ship it to Flanders themselves. In the last short while, refugees who fled the mortality in the Low Countries came to Essex and Kent. I met one who said he used to make cloth in Bruges. Why do we not use our money to raise sheep, build a mill and make the cloth ourselves? Tending a herd of sheep calls for much less labour than ploughing and reaping crops – just a few men are needed to tend a flock and wool is much more profitable than growing beans or onions. And, we have the grasslands of Kent and eastern England to feed the long-woolled flocks.'

Jude looked hesitant. 'What do we know about spinning and weaving?' he asked plaintively.

Joseph nodded. 'We don't know much but we will be able to sell our product, and we'll have money to hire those who do,' he said. 'Getting the wool is fairly simple. You shear the sheep and separate the wool into grades for spinning. The coarser fibres make worsted yarn; the softer, inner layers make woollen yarn.

'There are processes to clean, rinse and disentangle the wools, to dye, grease and comb them and then they need spinning, knitting or weaving before the finishing processes like fulling and napping the fabric are performed. It's not magical. It just needs skilled workers. With our French gold we already have enough money to hire people and to build a fulling mill for the cleansing and thickening processes. All of this can be done on a small scale for, say, a single family in an ordinary home but if you want to make a business of it – and that can be very profitable – you need more than a spinster or two and some walker to pound the cloth underfoot.'

I spoke my thoughts aloud: 'I'd rather do that than break my back cutting rows of grain with a hand sickle.'

Henry laughed. 'I can see myself as a wealthy weaver, Tom, but what about Jude – would he make a pretty spinster?'

Joseph snorted. 'We're here and alive despite everything. We're none of us dyers!' And we all laughed. After such dark days of war, plague and death, we seemed at last to have a future worth anticipating.

The very next day, I met someone to share that future – a dark-haired young widow called Alice, a broderer who also acted as her own marleywoman. 'I embroider fine clothes and I make marli. It's a fabric into which you sew the embroidery,' she explained. I did not take in a word of what she said. I was entranced, gazing at her eyes and mouth, dazzled by her even white teeth and itching to hold her slender body. She stamped her foot in pretended annoyance and pouted. 'Tom! You are not listening to me!'

I protested that I was thinking about our proposed cloth business and wondering how to include fine embroidery on our goods. She looked at me with suspicion. 'Joseph will deal with that problem,' she said, tartly.

I looked across at him, for he had brought Alice to meet his brothers and me. He gave me a cool look, said, 'She's right, Tom. Alice knows,' then grinned broadly. He knew I was smitten.

Six days later, I proposed to marry her; two months after that, once the banns were called at our local parish church (although only four people were there to hear them) we were married.

Time sped up its flow as we settled into a different, saddened life as the ravages and terrors of the Great Pestilence eased. We saw few people; we concerned ourselves with creating a cloth business, finding a water mill, growing our food – the days of plenty were gone, as there were so few people to work the land. Churchmen, knights, even aldermen had to plough, harvest and thresh for themselves if they wanted bread to eat, and they had no skills in the matter. Many nobles determinedly refused to work with their hands: it was simply unacceptable for them to demean themselves so much.

But they needed goods and food so the work fell on the peasants, of whom there were too few. And that class, instead of paying their rents with grain and crops, could and did demand money which the nobles reluctantly paid. They had no choice. It was no longer easy to find peasants to do the work and if the masters wouldn't pay, the peasants would move on until they found someone willing to pay proper wages.

Our Thatcher clan was among the fortunate. We had able-bodied men: the brothers Joseph, Henry and Jude as well as myself, all of whom had somehow – perhaps by going to war – escaped the plague. We had our wives and a few children of Joseph's who were old enough to help, even if it was only scaring off the starlings and other birds that raided our seeds and crops. We had enough labour to survive and some more to prosper, and we were well paid for it.

* * *

121

Another huge change in our lives was our acquisition of a water mill near Sittingbourne. The miller and his family had died a year before and we felt little danger that the plague still infested the place but we fumigated it, scrubbed everything and built some new cots for the cloth workers we hoped to attract. My booty from France helped and soon two Flemish weavers came through Bowerfield on their way to Dover: a man and wife with two children whose community in Essex had been ravaged by the pestilence so they had opted to return to Flanders. They were hungry and cold; Alice mothered the children and fed the parents and in a day or two they agreed to work for us and even to try to recruit other skilled clothworkers to do the same, an agreement that in time brought us a small but skilled body of workers.

Joseph saw how our enterprise was growing and proposed building a grain mill to operate off our millrace, too. In a year, we were fulling cloth and grinding grain, feeding our families and offering charity to the hungry and homeless. Our future looked bright. Or it did until the ailing King Edward again put his royal boot on the peasants' necks.

The king and his nobles and prelates in Parliament voted to enact the Statute of Labourers and obliged every peasant to swear to abide by it. This said in effect that we must work for no more than the miserly wages we had been grudgingly given before the plague, or labour for free, as before. Worse, we must not travel to find work elsewhere at better rates than the three pence a day set wage for harvesting: we were to remain on our baron's holdings and work only for him, as we did before the disaster of the Great Mortality. While we were still grumbling at this new imposition, further taxes were slapped on everyone above the age of fourteen but, essentially, they landed hardest on the poor. The nobility was trying to force the peasants back into what they regarded as our rightful place.

* * *

Soon after the taxes were announced by a hard-faced sheriff's man, two people who would have a great influence on our lives separately arrived at the gates of our mill. The first was a Welshman from the Isle of Anglesey. A shortish, thickset man with heavy black brows, he rode up on a fine bay mare, slid off his mount, asked for me and advanced with his hand outstretched in greeting. In a singsong voice, he announced himself: 'My name is Tudur ap Goronwy,' he said. 'I was a royal officer. I am just returning from service in King Edward's army in France and I heard of you from Robert Knollys, so I diverted from my journey to meet you.'

Tudur explained that he had inherited his grandfather's considerable lands in the north-west Wales island of Anglesey which included vast fields of wheat, rye and barley. These crops could find a profitable market in England. 'It would be easy to ship it from Conway or Caernarvon and bring it to you here, offload it for grinding and then sail the flour upriver to London's hungry market. Water all the way, see?' It was a venture not to be missed. His Welsh island had largely escaped the plague so there were labourers to gather the grain and we were in position to profit. We shook hands on the agreement and within a few months the first shipments began to arrive.

Something else, or rather someone else, arrived about the same time: a fiery priest called John Ball. A balding, scrawny man in a patched brown habit, he told us he had been ordained at York and had recently left Norwich, where he had worked in a lazar house for pestilence victims and had miraculously survived. He had no parish but preached in churchyards, usually to congregations leaving after Mass. That practice had brought him into conflict with the Archbishop of Canterbury, Simon Sudbury, who was not only England's most senior churchman but was also chancellor of the exchequer. 'His

Excellency has had me thrown into prison three times already,' he said calmly, 'and no doubt he will have it done again.'

Ball's contentious message was that all men are equal. 'God created no bondsmen, no slaves. Our servitude to the nobility began only through the actions of evil men. If God had wanted some men to be slaves or bondsmen and others to rule them, he would have decided who should be what, right from the beginning. These masters appointed themselves; they have no right to make you their servants. You can set aside your servitude, your so-called obligations to them. It is no sin to do so.' Whenever Ball delivered such a sermon – and he gathered crowds from Billericay in Essex to Waltham in Kent – the reaction was stunned disbelief, then indignation and, lastly, a declared resolve to confront their manorial lords that ebbed away when it came time to do it. Obviously, the common folk needed something to ignite their will. It took two other renegade priests, a bird trainer and a roof-mender to do it.

Oliver the falconer came to my cottage one evening at dusk. The bishop of Rochester's man had been with me that fateful night, just before I killed Ottercombe. Right after the killing I had fled, knowing there would be no mercy for the death of a manorial official, however accidental it was. He came, now, as one who had once been a serf but now was a miller and man of property, to help organise a guild or society of labourers to push the manorial lords into improving our wages and conditions.

'Remember me?' he asked, sardonically. I surveyed his stocky self and nodded.

'Aye, Master Falconer, through no fault of your own, you were a bird of ill omen the last time we spoke. I agreed with what you had to say but, minutes after we talked, evil befell me.' On reflection, I considered he could not have known that I'd faced Ottercombe just after he had left for Rochester, though it was likely he'd heard that I'd killed the fellow, so I added: 'These last few years since we spoke, I have had to be elsewhere and we have had war, plague and an ocean of troubles. I hope we are now moving into calmer waters.'

He sucked his teeth noisily. 'I'm not so sure I can confirm that. It's storms that change things. And, by the Virgin, we need some changes made!' I nodded and gestured to a bench I'd placed under a handsome beech tree, and there we sat and talked.

What Oliver had to say was encouraging. I knew for myself what first he spelled out: that the peasants were discontented and wanted change. What he told me next lifted my spirits. 'There are a number of rabble rousers wandering through Kent and Essex and even further north, to Lincoln and York, for example, but they are limited in their followings and even more limited in their abilities. However, educated men: clergy and aldermen, wealthy merchants and even members of the nobility who have a conscience are joining our movement and they can be persuasive, even leaders of our campaign to aid the common man.

'They agree that more is needed than just powerless pleading with those who leech off us. We need to demonstrate our own strength and will and for that we will need men with different skills than mere rabble-inciting. We will need men who can lead others, men who can organise resources, men who are unafraid. We need men who have military training and can make an unorganised mob into a deter-mined army if we are to demonstrate to our manorial lords that we are not puny, weak bondsmen. If we fail to demonstrate our strength, the barons will crush us to ensure we don't rise against them again.'

Oliver said bitterly: 'I don't know how it is here, but our bishop and his reeve rule with a rod of iron. They monitor us and earmark every yard of tilth for their purposes. Those who work certain holdings are responsible for cutting down trees and stacking his Grace's woodpile; others must take water to the haymakers, keep the irrigation ditches flowing freely and dig drainage where the marl is too heavy. Other holdings are designated for the manufacture of bell ropes for the parish church or make repairs to the church and its buildings. The shepherds and the bishop's servants – of whom I am one – are sustained by certain holdings. Others' tenants must build fences and take them down after harvest; or ensure that only an allotted number of cattle may graze on the common; or collect straw, rushes, sedge and reeds for the thatchers. The list goes on and on from those who must slaughter the beasts when winter comes to those who are delegated to butcher the meat, salt or smoke it and tan the hides.

'And, as if to emphasise how enslaved we are, our bishop has from time to time sold pieces of his land along with the cattle on it, also selling the very peasants who worked it. He values the people as little as he values his beasts and maybe even less than the animals in his fields. And you cannot leave. If you do depart the manor, you will be dragged back again. If your son wants to take up a trade, to become a priest or be a soldier, he must get special permission and that is not often given. Slaves are all we are and there is nothing in any holy book that says God made certain classes or groups of men to be enslaved. That is just the doing of selfish men, and even the king is doing it, offering peasants their freedom on payment of £15 – more than three years' wages.

'And did the church do anything to better the commoners' lot? Hardly, they were too busy leading the life of nobles. In Oxford we heard the canons of St Frideswide kept a pack of hounds; in Glastonbury, the abbot had a choice of five country houses and had appropriated twenty-one parish churches taking the tithes for himself while employing a single underpaid vicar to serve the faithful. In Bury St Edmunds, the abbot dined off silver plate and boasted of the outriders who accompanied him on his rounds as he travelled like a Caesar. 'These monks are robust men capable of honest work but they have declined manual labour and claim to have an ascetic ideal which they do not observe,' charged Oliver. 'They embezzle from their charities and they turn their hospices, which were intended to provide free shelter to pilgrims, into taverns for carousers.'

It was overwhelming to hear all this and know it was true. I must have sounded despondent when I asked, 'So where do we go from here?'

Oliver lowered his voice. 'We spread the word; we tell people how we can improve matters. We build a brotherhood; we gather resources and arms against the time we will need them and we do it without the barons' or the bishops' knowledge so that when we act, they will not be ready to respond. We may need to fight, and surprise is a soldier's best friend. We need local leaders like you, who are respected and have military experience as well as some wealth.'

I heard the call and resolved to join the cause.

So, we began the long, slow process of forming a Great Company of peasants. In those early years of the process, the foundations were laid by men such as Oliver the falconer, and then the visionary John Ball, the so-called 'mad priest of Kent' who was our great inspiration with his fiery sermons and unbroken spirit despite the number of times the authorities captured and imprisoned him. Ball visited villages and did the preaching, telling people not to pay the tithes, predicting a future without lordship when a peasant would no longer have to labour in wind and rain and Christ would 'pay for all'.

That message was broadcast, too, by men such as Geoffrey Litster of Norfolk, Wat Tyler of Maidstone and the Oxford scholar John Wycliffe, who spread the word to build our Great Company. In our part of Kent, Owen Blackburn the leech gatherer was a messenger and aide to priests like Ball and the curate John Wrawe of Essex who preached and recruited followers across eastern England. Blackburn was especially useful as he had freedom to roam for his work and was not tied to a selion or two of land to grow crops, so his travels never aroused suspicion.

Others who helped organise companies of resentful peasants were workmen and itinerant artisans on the tramp to escape the strictures of compulsory work laid down in the Statute of Labourers. They went from village to village seeking work, evangelising and spreading discontent. So too did religious mendicants, full-time vagrants, broken men of all kinds and outlaws carrying the sanction of the Wolf's Head: an edict that they were criminals liable without punishment to the same treatment as that meted to a dangerous, wild creature. For all that, they were men who often had been treated harshly.

Nor were the malcontents limited to those who worked the land. Townsmen discontented with their feudal superiors wanted to extract more favourable terms and charters from them and supported their rural cousins. Most frequently, the objects of resentment were churchmen, for abbots and bishops who were landowners were notoriously slow to concede rights to their tenants, dues which even the king and his grasping nobles had granted for the past couple of centuries. Astute townsmen recognised that in a time of anarchy, reluctant clergy would be more likely to agree to new charters and freedoms when lawlessness was rampant, so they, too, joined our campaign.

During these years of quiet meetings in churchyards, of surreptitious gathering of weapons and money, Alice and I, with the help of four Flemish weavers – our original recruits, Roland and Karin, had brought two more of their cousins – ran our wool business and fulling mill while Jude and Joseph and their families managed the grinding mill to which Tudur ap Goronwy sailed cargoes of Welsh grain. We did a side business in linen, a fabric woven from flax fibre, and a small trade in cotton from France and Flanders.

Free from feudal obligations, we prospered and saw for ourselves how the great monasteries had become so wealthy and so removed from their true purpose. Restless villagers obliged to work for pittances had already rioted against the great abbeys at Vale Royal, Bury St Edmunds, Abingdon and St Albans; priests had been attacked by peasants, and tax collectors murdered by knights. We made sure we dealt fairly with our suppliers and clients and followed Christ's injunction to feed the hungry, and all the while we quietly promoted our gospel of the equality of all men and the injustices of church and state.

During this turbulence, the ailing King Edward's mistress, Alice Perrers, became England's richest woman through royal land grants and corrupt influence-peddling to secure legal decisions in her friends' favour. She was so blatant that Parliament passed laws forbidding women from practicing in the courts of law, but she continued to flaunt her wealth, presiding at tournaments lavishly dressed and decked in ropes of pearls while the common people grumbled about her as they suffered through weather-ruined crops and near-starvation.

Even Oxford scholars bubbled with discontent. On St Scholastica's day, two ordained clergymen complained about the quality of wine served to them in the Swindlestock Tavern. A quarrel with the taverner and his friends aroused old resentments between town and gown and a melée began with locals and students facing off against each other. Rioting broke out; reinforcements began to arrive for each side. Violence continued for three days until armed gangs hired by the town bailiffs marched in from the surrounding countryside to support the townspeople, raid the university and halls and murder the student defenders. About 2,000 weapons-carrying rustics arrived under a black flag, crying 'Havoc!' to loot the university and hunt down students. Much of the town was burned down, some twenty taverns and halls were sacked and about a hundred people from both sides were killed. Several tonsured clerics were reported to have been scalped and student corpses were dumped in cesspits or dunghills or thrown into the Thames.

The king sent judges to determine the course of events and to punish wrongdoers. The inquiry held for the university; the townspeople were fined; the mayor and bailiffs were imprisoned and the bishop of Lincoln put the city under interdict for a year, banning masses, burials and marriages. An additional penalty was levied: as an annual penance, the mayor, bailiffs and sixty townsfolk of Oxford were obliged to attend a memorial Mass each year on the anniversary of the riot. A royal charter also fixed the rights of the university above those of the town, including assigning the chancellor the power to tax food and drink sold in the town and to oversee assay weights and measures.

The news travelled to us in Kent, where the resentful rumbles against the landlord barons and bishops continued to grow louder. We knew that the king's mistress, Alice Perrers, had dishonestly become the richest woman in England, flaunted her wealth and had been barred from the courts for corruption. The old king Edward burdened us with heavy taxes for wars and although his expenditure to build Queenborough Castle was steep, we forgave it, for the fortress on the River Swale was important to the wool trade, guarding as it did the seaway to the Channel. Nor did we men of Kent grumble when the Wool Staple, which required overseas trade in certain goods be conducted in a designated centre, was moved there from Canterbury. To my wife Alice and I, building our wool business, it seemed that maybe trade and prosperity might soothe the discontent but other storm clouds were gathering.

Then the tempest broke. A king's messenger rode into our village with the announcement: all men sworn to military service were to report to Southampton Castle by St Anselm's Day in April and be prepared to join Prince Edward's mounted expedition in France. Having shouted his shocking news, he galloped away to stir up the next village. I sighed. This, I knew would mean a half year away from my wife, our mill and our peaceful life. I took down my harness and weapons and began cleaning them.

Chapter 18

Chevauchée

Prince Edward of Woodstock had led his army on a great mounted raid 100 leagues across France in two months of looting, burning and fighting. His force of archers captured five walled towns and seventeen castles, devastated more than 500 villages and scorched the earth and its crops across a region that usually sent annual tribute of more than 400,000 golden coins to their king. The English took so much booty they threw away mere silver so the 300-wagon train which carried the loot could be filled with stolen gold, jewels, carpets, clothes, armour and wall hangings.

Edward sent the loot back to England and celebrated a lavish Christmas in Aquitaine while the French peasants shivered and starved in roofless, ruined hovels set in charred fields and cursed the overlords who had not driven out the Black Boars. Then, the prince planned to do it all again. He called his Gascon war lords to council on the Feast of the Epiphany and outlined his ideas for a three-pronged campaign.

The prince was to strike from Gascony. Edward himself would rampage through Brittany and Henry de Grosmont, the fighting

Duke of Lancaster, was to wreak havoc in Normandy and draw the French away from the Black Prince's campaign further south. In the late spring, we briefly rode out again. We started well, raiding thirty leagues up the Garonne and taking the town of Castelsagrat. One of my archers, Andrew of Leatham, killed the captain of that town by putting an arrow through his head at 120 paces, a feat which earned him a small barrel of cider and the plaudits of his admiring fellows.

We left a strong force of men-at-arms and Lombardy mercenaries to garrison the town and they used it as a base from which to raid across the region. Even our diet improved. During the previous winter's chevauchée, we had existed on salt beef and whatever fresh meat we could scoop up on the raid, but from our garrisons we could purchase meat, fish, poultry and grains as well as onions and garlic. Prince Edward invited me to sup and I was impressed to see that his cook brought fruit, almonds, eels, oysters and honey to the table to supplement the fine venison and beef. Soon, we returned to our stronghold and readied for a Great Raid. First, though, my literacy proved useful to the prince: I was tasked with establishing advance depots along the Garonne and with overseeing the various clerks and their spectrum of duties.

And it was a spectrum of skills: the clerk of the marshalcy disbursed payment to farriers and smiths for shoeing horses and paying grooms' wages; the office of the buttery was responsible for the purchase and transport of wine; the office of the poultry bought hens and eggs; the clerks of the kitchen and pantry oversaw our supplies of meat, cheese, fish and wheat; the saucery dealt with vegetables and precious spices; the clerk of the scullery handled purchasing and transporting fuel, specifically coal and firewood as well as herbage for the animals; and the office of the hall had a variety of duties including transporting the prince's personal items and building temporary cabins for the gentry. Last came the spicery, whose cashier handled wages, the prince's own expenses, donatives and reparations and any money owed to individuals.

So, the summer began in a blizzard of lists and requisitions and, after some weeks, it was with vast relief I heard Edward say: 'Tom, put away your quills and grease your harness. We'll be on the move shortly. I'm hoping to be ready by St Thomas' Day.'

Hmm, I thought, early July. The year was 1356.

'We're to aid my father's Norman allies and wreak some havoc along the way.'

And we did. More or less on schedule, on the eve of the Translation of St Thomas a Becket, we left La Réole, just as Lancaster began his forays to the north. Between us, we devastated Limousin, Berry and Auvergne, scorched the countryside and hanged the survivors of any garrison which resisted us.

And King John sought revenge. Our scouts first reported that he seemed to be lost and had marched his men in a wide circle, seeking us; then he was marching parallel to us with 55,000 men to our 8,000; they had destroyed the bridges over the Loire, denying Lancaster passage to join us and, worse, King Edward's fleet had been blockaded and trapped so he could not join us, as planned, at the Loire.

We were outnumbered seven to one, our nearest refuge was in Gascony, an impossible hundred leagues away and our hopes of reaching and taking a walled town where we could hold out had just been shattered. The French had crossed the one remaining bridge and stood squarely in our way. Then came news that the Comte d'Armagnac had plucked up his courage and had begun attacking English-held towns in Gascony. Our Gascon troops immediately wanted to go home to defend their territory. They left, weakening still further our already underpowered force.

Prince Edward called a council and announced that even the town of Poitiers, a mere league distant, was out of our reach. We must fight and it would not be easy. We remembered the lessons of Crecy and of Dupplin Moor: to find ground difficult for the enemy to cross *en masse*; to protect our flanking archers from their cavalry and to force the enemy through choke points on the battlefield so they could not deploy the full weight of their army at any one time. At those two previous battles, more men died under their comrades' trampling feet than died by hostile weapons, for the enemy were pressed from behind by legions of soldiers struggling through narrowing gaps; men stumbled and fell to be crushed and suffocated.

Heavy weather moved in, just as our scouts went out to survey the area, and we heard distant rumbles of thunder. The rain began lashing down and our archers unstrung their longbows and hid the bowstrings under their hats to keep them dry. Edward chose to establish our army on a half-mile long ridge that rose south and east of the city and faced a broad valley. The ridge was contained in a loop of the Moisson River, which sat in a ravine among much broken ground and provided protection against attack from the rear. Across the river was the town and abbey of Nouaillé, where we blocked a bridge with farm carts. The rising ground over which the French must advance was broken up by small orchards and thick hedges of thorn which offered excellent protection for our archers. Even the 'open' ground was cluttered with entangling brambles and patches of vines that would slow their cavalry.

On one flank, the dense St Peter's Wood provided further defences against cavalry; on the other wing a steep escarpment offered security.

To the front, some sunken lanes, small orchards and strong hedges promised to seriously hinder attacking cavalry from gaining full impetus. Two tracks that led to us diverged from a point where the French front rank took stance. The easterly one, on our right flank, ran right through an especially prominent stout and thick hedge that would make a fine stand for our archers and we viewed it covetously. Prince Edward arrayed his two battles of infantry on either side of the other track. Our front was the strongest natural position available and we began reinforcing it with trenches, tree trunks and sharpened stakes set in front of the hedges, then placed our forces behind their screen. We also set heavy, pointed stakes among the archers' ranks, angling them upwards as a deadly hedgehog to impale cavalry horses. Knollys planned to have archers stand among them, to conceal them from the enemy until they were almost upon us. All the while we were digging and setting, we watched as King John's army was mustered and aligned a mile away. The rain ended and a blazing sun emerged, setting the battleground steaming.

The French formed three divisions: King John heading one battle, his son Philip another and the Dauphin Charles commanding the vanguard. Aware of the vulnerability of their horses to English arrows, John ordered his knights and men-at-arms to dismount and to fight on foot. A fourth small division of cavalry held the centre in front of the three large divisions and was flanked west and east by crossbowmen. 'They're not so many as they might be,' Prince Edward remarked to Knollys as we surveyed the enemy host. 'My scouts tell me they left a lot of infantry behind in their hurry to pass us. I'd say they don't have much more than two or three times our numbers.' He paused thoughtfully. 'Better yet, what they do have, they've deployed badly.'

The French main army was arrayed in three large battalions aligned behind each other, which meant that only the front rank could do any actual fighting. Worse for them, John's decree that almost all his knights should dismount and fight on foot meant that their advance in heavy armour would be so much slower, especially through the muddy ground, and would subject them much longer to the withering arrow storms we would send their way.

Slow and badly aligned or not, our own formation seemed puny by comparison to the enemy's. Two battles of English and Gascon foot soldiers, each division only about the size of the fourth and smallest French formation, formed our front and were flanked left and right by Welsh and Cheshire longbowmen. Behind them stood about 400 English cavalry. The prince nodded agreement when Knollys suggested putting the archers on the right flank behind the thick thorn hedge and he angled them slightly to have a clear field of fire into the left wing of the oncoming French.

I readied myself for the fighting and took stock of my own gear: linen braies as underclothes and a padded aketon over my torso to reduce the chance of a spear thrust pushing broken metal into my flesh. Next was a knee-length mail shirt called a hauberk. Its neck pulled up into a hood and had a lined flap that could be tied to protect the throat and lower face. The whole thing was laced tight to keep it snug and I wore leather-soled mail leggings over thick woollen socks.

My outer layer of protection was formed by breast and back plates hung on a harness, with shin and foot guards laced over my mail stockings and gauntlets to protect my hands. As we would be fighting on foot, it was lighter, more supple equipment than I would use when fighting from horseback, and I chose a brimmed sallet helmet that gave me better peripheral vision, to help in the hand-to-hand brawls we expected.

In front of me, our longbowmen were busily sticking arrows in the ground in front of their stands, enabling faster reloading and adding to the lethality of their barbs – a dirtied wound would be infected. Behind me, a steady stream of noncombatants shuttled back and forth bringing up sheaves of 144 arrows at a time in their willow-wand-reinforced linen bags which kept the fletchings from being crushed. The archers all carried spare bowstrings, kept tucked inside their caps, and most of the bowmen planted a spear or sword by their stand in case the enemy broke through.

A burst of jeers and booing broke out from our ranks. The French had raised a slender red and gold pennant on a golden staff. 'The Oriflamme, Tom,' said Rob Knollys, who had come to stand by me. 'Their signal that no prisoners will be taken. It's supposed to terrify us.'

'I wouldn't want to be a prisoner of the French,' I said. 'Having to eat snails and garlic.'

He laughed. 'Edward and a couple of knights parlayed with some churchmen and King John earlier. John said he'd crush us. Edward smiled at him and said our archers would shoot them flat but he was willing to return any "lost" valuables we had saved for them – if John would agree to a seven-year truce to allow his people to recover from the unfortunate damage.'

'And?' I asked.

'John wanted one hundred knights and the prince to ransom themselves. Edward politely declined and John stormed off.'

Rob Knollys tugged at his ear reflectively. 'John's outsmarted himself. He delayed battle to allow more of his troops to arrive but they're just now dragging themselves in, exhausted. We had time to reinforce our defences; they arrived footsore and tired from marching fast in full armour. Look how slowly they're coming up the slope.'

I also observed what he did not say: that the French showed their inexperience as well as their fatigue. They advanced in a way that meant only their front ranks could fight – the rest trailed along behind. Our hardened, fighting Black Boars had been campaigning across France for two years; they were tough, experienced, mobile and confident. They were also going to fight like devils to protect their loot. We might be well outnumbered but we were not an inferior force.

Below us, the French seemed to straggle reluctantly onwards and they took an inordinate amount of time to plod up the semi-sunken roadway under the slopes of the ravine that was the most viable point of attack. Our archers were stationed on the wings of our battle line; we could sight on the French flanks and fire into the near-unprotected sides of their war horses – which our bowmen did to great effect.

The day became a repetition of the familiar twanging song of 2,000 bowmen simultaneously releasing their bowstrings; of the whistle of the grey goose-feather flights as the spinning arrows arced high and slammed down at a steep angle intended to hit men's heads and shoulders so there was little to shield them. And, those downpours of steel broadhead and bodkin points were launched six or eight times a minute. Soon the arrows ceased to fall in waves and flights; they became a continuing, constant storm of steel-tipped ash smashing through iron, leather and cloth and into human flesh at the speed of a plummeting peregrine. The day became one of thrashing, screaming, agonised horses; bellowing, sobbing men; of the merged stink of dung, vomit, crushed grass and mud and the salt smell of blood.

A few of the French knights spurred their horses close to the archers. The archers stepped back through the ranks of English spearmen who themselves stood behind the protective rows of pits and sharpened stakes that impaled the chests of the maddened horses and hurled their riders onto the men-at-arms' pitiless spearpoints. For all of those brave knights who made it close, thousands did not. They advanced so slowly they were exposed to the withering volleys of arrow fire for a hundred or more steady heartbeats and died in their hundreds. As they fell, their comrades behind them slowed and, in turn, were pressed onwards by the mass of the army trying to force its way through the chokepoints both natural and created by us.

Pressed from behind, blocked by the dead and dying in front, the ranks became a mob, stumbling and dying under the boots of their comrades. And, all the time, the merciless missiles thumped into them. John Chandos commanded our cavalry and saw his chance. He led a powerful charge into the French flank and shattered the entire attack. The men-at-arms turned and ran; their knights hauled back their mounts and spurred them away, trampling their own soldiers as they fled. In minutes the battle turned into a swirl of small groups of combatants, the French trying to escape, the English eager to capture someone worth ransoming. And the conflict dragged wearyingly on, with fatigued men dragging themselves out of the combat to rest and suck down water before wading back into the press of men brutally hacking and jabbing at each other. Gradually, the battering eased, the shouting, grunting mob quieted and the French began easing away, slipping through their own mob to try to snag a horse and escape.

Chapter 19

Aftermath

The battlefield was a butcher's shop, with swathes of eviscerated corpses oozing purple and pink intestines, shattered skulls spilling white-grey brains and here and there a cadaver looking calm and peaceful, apparently unwounded. Looters were combing the field. If they found a living opponent, they usually beat him unconscious to allow his armour and goods to be stolen more easily. One body of English men-at-arms were supervising a large group of prisoners to dig burial pits in the form of spiral holes with down and up ramps to facilitate burying the multitudes of corpses.

Over here, surgeons and apothecaries inside a corral of baggage wagons were working on wounded Englishmen. Their procedures looked rough and painful but I learned they had potions made of boar gall, briony, opium, henbane, vinegar and hemlock which, taken with a draught of wine, induced sleep while the surgeon did his bloody business. Some surgeons used a fleam to bleed the already-wounded patient. They inserted a narrow blade to open a vein and the fleam allowed the blood to flow through a channel in the handle. The commonest wounds included arrow strikes, which posed bad problems. War arrowheads are sometimes attached only with warm beeswax which, when set, allows the arrow to be used normally. Once shot into something, however, the head will detach once the shaft is tugged and the metal is left in its target.

A surgeon taking a breather from his butchery showed me an answer to the problem of removing an arrow that could not simply be pushed all the way through its victim's flesh. 'It's a sort of narrow spoon,' he explained, 'that we can insert into the wound and wrap around the arrowhead to draw it from the body without causing further damage as the barbs rip out. Once the arrowhead's removed, we cauterise the wound with red hot irons to seal the veins and flesh to prevent blood loss and infection.' I gulped and thought pityingly of the man-at-arms undergoing his time on the table, thanked the surgeon and walked away, feeling faintly sick.

Away from the killing ground, the prince had chased the French to the gates of Poitiers where an eddy of fighting clashed around the blue banner of King John under which a rank of his red-clad royal bodyguard lay dead. The Oriflamme went down; John, who was swinging a great war axe, was captured and surrendered his gauntlet to Sir Denis de Mortbeque of Artois, who handed it to the prince in his red silk pavilion under an elm behind our position. That ended the fighting which chroniclers said caused 3,000 dead.

Our men took for ransom about 1,500 wealthy knights plus another 100 counts, barons and bannerets and within a week we had sent the captive French king to London. There he was paraded in triumph through the city to the Savoie Palace where he languished, awaiting the arrival of his ransom: four million gold crowns, or twice the annual income of France. That nation could not pay and John would eventually die in England.

King Edward could view his achievements with satisfaction. He had John of France under his control; David of Scotland was also held fast at Windsor Castle and a regency was installed in Edinburgh to gather his ransom. The pestilence was easing, trade was expanding and England was prospering. Below the surface, however, a new society to replace the old regime was fermenting.

I was not in England to enjoy the new prosperity, however. Word had reached me that my wife Alice had died in childbirth; even the baby, a girl, was dead. I had no wish to return to our Kent mill. I could not face seeing the place where we had been so happy. Rob Knollys found me in the Poitiers house I had commandeered and two days later I was riding with him and his 2,000-strong army of freebooters.

'With John in chains, there's a throne up for grabs and much gold to be gathered, Tom,' he told me. 'Charles of Navarre and his brother Philip have a mind to give the Dauphin the boot and take away the crown he's waiting to wear. It's good for our king: Edward wants Aquitaine back; it supports his claim to be king of France. So, anything we can do to help our king and the Spaniards, too, will be patriotic and, by the way, it will make us rich!'

It began a blurred time in my life. I was grieving for Alice, burning and killing for Edward and looting for myself. We scorched the Loire Valley, a place of castles and wealth and we left so many burned buildings behind us that their ruined gables were being called 'Knollys' Mitres.' I recall names like Chateauneuf-val-de-Bargis where we set up a garrison as an advance supply dump and strongpoint for Charles' invasion; we besieged the Burgundy city of Auxerre and captured it despite its new walls. The prince celebrated the victory by knighting Knollys, so he became Sir Robert.

'A pleasant step up from being a squire, my lord,' I joked with him. Rob grinned.

'As long as we keep the gold coming, you can call me anything, Tom.'

Auxerre was once a Roman city, had an ancient cathedral, an abbey and several churches and was wealthy through the wine trade. I learned much about sacking a city there. 'We make the most money we can from this place,' Knollys said. 'No destruction, just some careful questions of the locals to see who has what and who can raise ransoms. If they want to keep their city, they must pay.' It was a sight to see: English men-at-arms and mounted archers at street corners or in the cathedral cloisters, watching over queues of citizens who waited to answer questions and demonstrate their wealth or lack of it, to be assessed a fine or pay a ransom. We learned to look up chimneys, to search out loose floorboards and to dig in the corners of gardens to find hidden loot and we found plenty.

Every English or Gascon soldier seemed to have a knapsack that chinked with coin, and then Rob – Sir Robert Knollys, I reminded myself – amassed another fortune. 'I've been told to put together an army, Tom,' he said over a jug of red Burgundy wine. 'The king's giving me some large land grants in Devon and a chest of gold coin to raise an army and invade northern France. He wants castles taken and churches reinforced so, when he brings his own army, he'll have strongpoints and supply depots already in place, just as the Black Prince did before our *chevauchée*. The Black Boars will be scouring the land again!'

But not everything went our way over the next several years. We freebooters briefly held Paris, attempted to take Avignon and ranged widely between the rivers Loire and Sarthe, ravaging, burning and looting as we went. In three weeks, we covered a gruelling thirty-three leagues, relieved and resupplied two towns under siege by the French and seized vast quantities of plunder. We even captured and destroyed a French siege train, wrecking their ability to retake the towns we had relieved.

Despite the list of successes, there was dissent among the various noble commanders who looked down on Knollys' humble origins and our army divided into several parts. Winter was coming, a powerful French army threatened us at the River Sarthe and Knollys wanted to retreat into Brittany. The other commanders refused, desirous of continuing their raiding to accumulate even more loot. I went with Rob and saved my life. Most of those who stayed were surprised by the French and butchered on St Ambrose Eve. The news of 3,000 English dead came to us in Brittany and I decided my time in France should end. I wanted the life of a civilian and a quiet life at that. Soldiering no longer appealed, so I took my loot, left France and made my own way back to Kent.

A couple of months later, under threat from a large French army, Rob Knollys tried to evacuate his own troops as well as the remnants of the forces defeated at the Sarthe. The English had too few ships but, dangerously overloaded, sailed anyway. They were forced to leave most of our men on the shore, where they were slaughtered. King Edward found Knollys responsible for the disaster, stripped him of the land grants that were his fee for the campaign and fined him 5,000lbs of gold.

When, months later, I heard the news, I was working in our fulling mill and I gave thanks to God that I was not a soldier. I would most likely have been killed at the bridge over the Sarthe or left dead on that bloodied beach at Sainte-Mathieu.

Sadly, during this time, my cousin Joseph, oldest of the Thatcher clan, succumbed to the plague. We buried him with sadness, his caring fidelity a huge loss to us.

Life continued more peacefully for a while. But for all the rural tranquillity of Kent, undercurrents were still moving powerfully. Two of them arrived together at my mill one beautiful spring morning when the sky was eggshell blue and the blossoms made every orchard a bee-buzzing flower garden.

The cloaked figures of two men, one an obvious cleric, the other bearing the familiar face of Wat Tyler, strode down alongside the millrace to greet me.

'Well met, Master Thatcher,' said Wat.

'Well met indeed, Walter, my friend,' I said, recalling the young man whose sister had died, leading him to a new faith: to change the order of things.

'This,' said Wat, indicating his balding, scrawny companion, 'is Father John Ball.' I saw from the man's worn brown habit that he was a cleric, but the name gave me a small start. He was known as a rousing orator, a firebrand follower of the preacher John Wycliffe, whom I had heard was imprisoned yet again for demanding church reform.

'I am happy to meet you, Father,' I said, extending a hand. 'Can I help, and have you broken your fast?'

Wat shook his head eagerly; Ball politely murmured that if there was a crust... and I called for Karin to prepare something: she helped run the mill and had acted as housemother since my wife Alice had died.

Over a small beer, fresh bread and ripe cheese, Wat and Father John explained matters. They had been at a private meeting in

Canterbury where Wycliffe was speaking and had chanced upon each other again in Maidstone, Wat's new home. The tiler, having had time to digest Wycliffe's ideas, had become an enthusiastic supporter of John Ball.

'We are not exactly Lollards,' said Ball quickly, then, as I frowned, explained the term. 'Father Wycliffe is a theologian and scholar who teaches that Christianity can be improved by better knowledge of the scriptures so his followers worship by reading them aloud. It sounds like they are muttering their prayers. Some have used the Dutch word "*lollebroeders*" or "mutterers" to describe Wycliffe's congregation, who pray for and bury the victims of the Great Pestilence.'

I wanted to be clear. 'You are not Lollards but you agree with Father Wycliffe?'

Wat spoke first. 'For myself, knowledge of the scriptures is less important than seeing the church reformed. They have become separated from their true purpose and preach one thing but practice another. They seem to wish only to accumulate wealth here on Earth but they preach that we their flock should concentrate only on saving our souls and gathering spiritual wealth in heaven. It seems they want to eat off gold and silver plate but Christ ate off wooden platters.

'Every pardoner or beadsman seems to have a different wench in each town; every monk ordered by St Benedict to live plainly and not eat certain things at certain times shrugs the injunction aside and says it only applies if they eat in the monks' refectory, so he may eat meat during Lent if he eats it in the cloister or in the chapter house.'

The duo spoke of monks who had to be forbidden to sing songs in taverns or to stop attending dances. They had to be warned not to entertain their relatives in the monastery, to stop keeping hawks or

practising archery. Some toured the countryside with portable altars
to attract donations or held confessions where the faithful could pay
for absolution. 'It's just scandalous,' said Tyler.

Wat's vehemence made me nod. We had all heard how the clergy
eased around the rules of fasting by classifying things conveniently for
themselves. Beavers were considered to be fish because they swam; the
small flagon of wine allowed each day was supplanted with unlimited
gallons of beer because the good saint had not specified rules for beer.
Wat was speaking again: 'On normal, non-fasting days, monks ingest
a couple of gallons of beer, five or six eggs, a 2lbs loaf of bread and
2lbs of fish or meat. That's nearly three times what a peasant doing
heavy labour consumes.'

Father Ball spoke up: 'As a spiritual exercise of self-restraint, for
about one-third of the year the church forbids the consumption of
the flesh of four-footed animals or even of animal products like eggs,
milk, cheese and butter. The wily monks seem, however, to have
found many legalistic loopholes and other ways to circumvent the
sumptuary laws and their dietary commandments.

'Offal, bacon or other processed meat is adjudged by the abbot
to be exempt from the rule. Fish, usually cod, pike or herring, is not
restricted, which opens the door to eating marine animals, so the
monks find themselves facing a feast that includes beaver tails, conger,
puffin breasts, oysters and roast barnacle goose.

'One elderly monk confided that they had even eaten whale when
I asked him about the dietary restrictions. "It is allowed," he said. I
was aware that noblemen eat non-meat meals, using fake eggs made
of fish roe with almonds and that they use similar cuisine trickery
to serve faux ham or venison during fast days, but I was taken aback
that the religious would circumvent the sumptuary edicts. The monks

say: "Brothers who are unwell are exempt from fasting, so they may partake of meat at all times, but generally the restrictions only apply to the refectory where we normally take our meals. If we eat elsewhere, the restrictions do not apply."'

I heard Father Ball out, then asked him quietly: 'Are you demanding reform just to stop gluttonous monks?'

He shook his head. 'I want the whole church to reform. I was ordained in York and believe in the stated principles of Mother Church. I believe all men are created equal and have spread that message widely, much to the annoyance of my lord Archbishop Simon of Sudbury, who has had me imprisoned four times and excommunicated once. Of course, I am also forbidden to preach. I admire the work of the Rector of Lutterworth, John Wycliffe. He is a scholar, philosopher, reformer and theologian and is also a professor at the University of Oxford. He questions the privileges to which the clergy consider themselves entitled and he decries the pomp and luxury afforded to parish clergy who often are barely even literate enough to say a Mass except to chant it by rote.'

Wycliffe's goal, Ball told me, was to translate the scriptures into English and to somehow get copies disseminated so that all could read them. This I personally found ambitious, as few outside the nobility and the clergy were literate. But the message that all men were equal in God's eyes was provoking. 'Does Father Wycliffe have support from any but the common people?' I asked.

Ball nodded. 'Many nobles resent the wealth, arrogance and land holdings of the church. They might not dissent about theology, if any of them understand enough to do so, but a number of knights at the king's court are anti-cleric and have been since the time of Becket and the church's insistence on its rights over their king's. I have heard that since Prince Edward died, his brother John, Duke of Lancaster, is sympathetic to that faction at court.'

That caused me to raise an eyebrow. John of Gaunt, the latest Duke of Lancaster, was a royal prince and one of England's wealthiest and most powerful nobles. The king was ailing, his heir Prince Edward was already dead; the next in line, the prince's son Richard was just a child of nine. John of Gaunt, an unpopular figure, would be acting as regent if matters proceeded as seemed likely and he could easily become king. This would be a shock for the common people, who knew him as a high-handed, incompetent, losing general who cost them a fortune in taxes levied for his campaigns. The peasants claimed he was the son of a Ghent butcher, a charge which reportedly infuriated him.

Wat the tiler was speaking and I jerked myself back from my musings. 'We have to bring our grievances to our local lords,' he said. 'Since the Great Pestilence, they have been increasing their control over us peasants.' I nodded agreement. I knew that new laws to which every man must swear obedience forbade peasants from leaving their parish to seek work elsewhere. I knew, too, that a peasant who wanted to buy his freedom so he could travel to find work must pay the ever-grasping crown the huge sum of £15: three years' pay for a skilled carpenter, seven years' pay for a labourer. Those who broke their oaths and took to tramping the region for work were dragged to court where part of the fines went to those who bought franchises to try such cases, making it in their interest to find peasants guilty and enrich both themselves and the crown. 'There can't be justice,' Wat said.

'There can,' Ball said grimly. He looked steadily at both of us. 'There will be justice because we will unite. Solidarity works for all. If we stand together, we are more powerful than any king or pope.'

Chapter 20

Committed

Karin the weaver came running into our watermill. 'There's fighting in the village!' she shouted. 'Come and help!' I grabbed my quarterstaff, shouted for Roland and we ran to see. We were soon joined by Jude and Henry, who had been elsewhere on the land but had heard the shouting. On the green, a gang of peasants had bloodied the reeve's two constables, who were slumped against a cottage under the guard of a handful of men armed with staves. More men were hacking with axes to destroy the stout stocks where two local men who had defaulted on their taxes were pinioned. We pushed our way through. My own standing as the local mill owner, plus the reputation we three Thatchers had as war-hardened Black Boars served to get us through and the axe men who were busily chopping up the stocks halted their work.

I recognised one man, a young and likeable shepherd called Ralph Banton and pointed my quarterstaff at him. 'You might have red hair, Ralph,' I said, 'but surely this is hot work even for you?'

The crowd murmured a laugh and Ralph grinned at the friendly tone. 'These fellows don't deserve to be in they-there stocks,' he said. 'They're fined and locked up for not bein' able to pay fines. That's not right.'

Privately, I agreed, but I said aloud: 'There's no call to beat the reeve's men, though. They're likely just doing what their master ordered them to do.' Addressing the crowd, I said: 'Best stop now what you're doing. Release these men and see to it that they are patched up. No more action against the constables, eh?'

A burly ploughman called Adam stepped forward truculently and addressed me: 'We do our jobs, too, Tom Thatcher, but we're still liable to heriots, game laws and enforced labour or we end up in chains or in the stocks like these poor devils. We want proper pay, proper food for our work. We're not slaves; we won't be beaten like animals anymore and we want to be allowed to seek work anywhere for proper pay and without the threat of being imprisoned for leaving our manor.'

I looked at him carefully. What he said made sense to me and I understood his grievances. 'You must speak to your lord, not to me,' I said shortly. 'I'm not the one imposing laws on you.'

He stepped forward, threateningly. 'You've got the water mill,' he said.

'Aye, that I have, and I earned it fighting in France. What have you done to earn a mill?'

'I didn't sell out to the king who taxes us,' he said, and hurled a meaty fist at me. I stepped back, swung my quarterstaff in a short arc and caught him on the temple. He dropped like a sack of flour.

A woman in the crowd called out: 'He deserved that. Adam's a bully. You did right, Tom.' An answering growl of approval went up.

I held out my hands, beseechingly. 'We're all in this together.

We're all subject to the king's taxes and tolls; we're all victims of the pestilence even if we didn't get it ourselves, because we have had to bury our dead and live without loved ones. The country is in ruins; the crops failed; we haven't the workers to harvest what little we did grow so our food is scarce and costs more. We need to rebuild with what we have, not to contest matters among ourselves. We need to make our masters treat us more fairly. We have to unite.'

A heavily bearded older man who looked like a prosperous merchant spoke up: 'In London, the tailors, the house painters and the filers have established guilds or brotherhoods that can withstand pressure from the church or nobility. It means they can earn two or three times the fees established by the law, or nobody will get their services.'

It made so much sense, I blurted out: 'That is exactly what we must do: organise ourselves and stand together. That way, we can make the king listen, however little he wants to hear what we have to say. We'll make him listen.' It did not sound like treason but it was enough. I had condemned myself, committed myself to an uprising. I'd declared against my king. May God help me.

In fact, He did not. The Great Pestilence returned and life got harder. King Edward's lawmakers wrote statutes that pegged wages at pre-plague prices, providing nobles and churchmen with a supply of cheap, even free, labour and slapped on a poll tax that everyone aged fifteen or more must pay because the king needed money to support his expensive foreign wars. The news arrived a week after my confrontation with Adam the ploughman, carried to us by Father John Ball. 'The church is not a good shepherd tending its flock: it is protecting its own interests,' he preached, and the peasants listened sourly. Some urged making our own king, saying that all we needed to do was to take the throne from Westminster – the throne with the sacred stone beneath it that the old king had stolen from the Scots – and hold our own coronation.

Then matters got even worse. The weather was bad; the crops were spoiled; locals came to our mill begging to be given flour we did not have to spare. We gave up to our fellow villagers some sacks of nuts, a whole bin of dried peas, two flitches of bacon and several tubs of salt-packed butter as well as a half dozen rounds of cheese. 'We can survive on what we have left – these families with children are desperate,' said Karin. 'They will not survive until spring without our help.' That said, she continued throughout the winter to have a pot of grain porridge bubbling for any hungry soul that came by.

Our hopes of reform were slim but John Ball preached to a crowd gathered outside the archbishop's palace in Canterbury, demanding that the church sell some of its treasures to buy food for the starving. Archbishop Sudbury sent his tipstaffs out to arrest the fiery priest, charged him with inciting a riot and imprisoned him again. It seemed our hopes of a better future were doomed.

It was at this time an unusual visitor arrived, having sailed on a Genoese cog into Queenborough where tax collectors were always posted to assess the cargo. The visitor was called Christian Bowdon and he had a remarkable tale to tell. It came out when he approached the king's reeve who was assessing the cargo and asked him in stilted English if he knew of Robert Knollys of Cheshire. The reeve looked over the questioner and saw a blond, bearded man. On his sun-bronzed cheek and forearm was branded an 'H' with a small circle on top.

'Knollys the freebooter?' the reeve had asked in surprise.

'Soldier, yes,' said the blond, eagerly.

The reeve was familiar with his district and recalled us, the

Thatchers, who had gone to war in France and famously returned with a fortune. 'There are some who may have served with him,' he had said cautiously. 'They own a water mill in Sittingbourne.'

So it was that Christian Bowdon arrived at our mill with a stunning tale to tell. Orphaned as a small boy, he had been cared for by his older brother Anthony and for lack of anywhere else to go, had accompanied him when Anthony was hired as an archer by a Genoese trader. The brother's profession as a mercenary took him to the trading post of Caffa and it was there during the second siege that the bowman was killed and the boy was captured by the Mongols. Jude and I even had dim memories of the event and of the general dismay that a popular young boy, whom we regarded as a sort of mascot, had gone missing.

'The Mongols were intrigued by my blond hair and thought it hilarious that I was a Christian whose name was Christian,' the man told us. 'I was their slave, so I was branded with these' – he gave a deprecatory shrug as he indicated the Turkic symbols on his face and arm – 'and after a year or two I was presented as a novelty to a Chinese warlord to be his personal servant. His name was Fang Guozhen and he was lord of the Zheng clan, which operated a huge fleet of salt trading, smuggling and pirate ships. I served on a few of the vessels when my master was aboard and I even went with him to the imperial court when he presented his captor, the Yuan emperor Zhu Yuanzhang the gift of all his fleet. In return, the emperor ennobled him and gave him a land grant of great size.'

Christian had some contact with the few European traders who dealt with the Yuan court and was helped by them to escape in exchange for smuggling jars of silkworms back to Europe – an export that could have cost him his head, for the Chinese held a jealous monopoly on the silk trade. Christian successfully made his way to the Black

Sea, to the Mediterranean and to Genoa. From there, with a reward for the silkworms and some stolen gold taken from the Yuans, he sailed with a trader to the Thames and came ashore in Kent nearly two decades after he left England. And he brought with him some explosive information.

Just as in Europe, the Great Mortality had ravaged China and two groups arose in rebellion after floods and famine also struck the region. The ruling Mongols did not deal well with the crises, and the peasants acted. Christian had close knowledge of how the Red Turban rebels of the north had joined with those of the south to promote insurrection; how they had organised; how they had ruthlessly carried out their uprising by killing key officials. 'I know the script to conduct an uprising,' he said simply. He was gold from heaven. We sat down to talk.

Christian spelled it out to Ralph Banton, who happened to be in the mill, to Roland the weaver and to me: 'You must have a clear purpose and explain to those who will follow you why the system is broken, how the king and his nobles are failing and what you wish to achieve. It is necessary that you have a proper action plan to include delegating responsibilities, to secure aid both physical and financial and to recruit partners. You'll need a leader, someone to inspire people or you may choose to act as a group, anonymously so the king cannot target that leader. It is best to have people in leadership roles who have different skills and techniques – you can't create an uprising with a single person.

'If there are signs and portents to interpret, be sure they foretell your success. We, too, have had years of plague that took away whole villages and left vast tracts of land unpeopled. We have seen stars streaking across the sky and the sun go dark at noon. We have had floods, extreme heat and extreme cold; crops have failed, and the population is starving. These things we have in common. They are all signs that God and the saints are displeased with the church and the king and, just as the Chinese people were justified in their resistance to their ruling Mongol oppressors, so you, too, are justified in an uprising.

'So, there are ways to dispense with bad rulers. It is good to have people inside the king's orbit. Identify sympathisers in his ranks and recruit them. Also identify key officials who must be eliminated to reduce the king's ability to strike back. Then match your strengths against your opponents' weaknesses, undermine them and demonstrate the breadth and strength of your movement and the numbers of the king's own subjects who now rage against him, demanding justice.

'Lastly, be prepared. Train to use military techniques to fight if you must use conflict: you have the population on your side; the king and his nobles only have some soldiers – and even they can be subverted.'

Ralph, the red-haired shepherd who had been a villein under the late Baron Roger's rule, spoke first: 'What we want is simple: an end to this being tied to our lord's land, an end to crippling taxes that are wasted on expensive wars and an end to feeding fat monks while we starve.'

I could not resist: 'We want to be men who are free of enforced labour, of chains and beatings. We want to be able to travel to find work where we wish and not to pay unreasonable demands for the basic acts of living. If the nobles and the church will not agree to demands like those, we'll just have to oust them. And I believe we can.'

That was how it really began: with the advent of someone who had witnessed bloody revolution in China, who had seen the Mongol overlords ejected and who gave us the ability to believe it could be done. I was deeply impressed, as one of the Thatcher clan who had witnessed at first hand the ferocity of the Mongols. If you could successfully rebel against them, their horse soldiers and their practised cruelties, other uprisings must be possible.

Chapter 21

Ironmaster

We began to spread the word with more determination through activists like Wat Tyler; the curate John Wrawe; the firebrand priest John Ball, who had just been released from prison again; the Oxford scholar-theologian John Wycliffe, a man of whom I at first was in awe and later came to value as a sensible, unselfish human genuinely dedicated to attempts to improve the rights of the commoner. And then there was a group of reformers who called themselves the Poor Preachers, whom I privately regarded as hysteric rabble rousers but useful to our cause anyway.

Men like Owen Blackburn the leech gatherer whom I also admired, went quietly about the countryside, telling of the building of a secret, new brotherhood. There was also the bishop's falconer, Oliver of Thanet, plus the Thatcher surviving cousins: Henry, Jude and myself and a widening network of neighbours, relatives and friends who all did what we could to broadcast the plan to improve all our lives and loosen or even discard the bonds of feudalism. For the old system was dying. After the Great Pestilence, a desperate need for labourers led some landowners secretly to pay more than the meagre levels set down by the crown. If they did not, many farmworkers like reapers or ploughmen formed unions to extort wages that were double or more above the crown's decree.

Angry peasants also protested, then rioted against wealthy, greedy clergy at the great abbeys of Bury St Edmunds, Vale Royal, St Albans and Abingdon. Some committed murders and assaults on priests, franklins and knights; there were attacks on tax collectors and struggling peasants refused to pay tithes to the church, arguing that they were already fined twice, at death. Then, the church took a man's second-best animal, saying the deceased had likely not paid enough tithes during his life, and the lord of the manor took the best animal to compensate for the military service the dead man could no longer perform. All knew it was unjust.

The rousing cleric John Ball travelled through Essex and Kent, preaching that corruption ruled both church and court, that parish priests knew the legends of Robin Hood better than they knew their scriptures. As for holy faith, sinful pilgrims took their sluts with them as they walked to the shrine at Walsingham; Ball charged friars with telling fake Bible stories to feed their fat bellies; he criticised lords who did not discipline their brutal men-at-arms; spoke of dishonest merchants who stretched their cloth or adulterated their goods and sold putrid meat, sour wine, or pepper dampened to weigh more. He called the church 'a dunghill covered in snow', pointed out that the young children of great men were often given fat livings as vicars of Christ; he so annoyed the authorities he was imprisoned again on the orders of Simon of Sudbury, Archbishop of Canterbury. The archbishop also excommunicated the rebellious priest and forbade anyone from hearing him preach.

Imprisoned or not, Father Ball's message spread widely and we reinforced it wherever we could. It did not take very long before visitors would slip into our mill and ask discreet questions about forming unions, brotherhoods, guilds or associations. We always answered without exaggeration and they usually left with thoughtful looks and hopeful eyes.

But we did more than talk. I travelled around the forests and ironstone quarries of Kent, discreetly seeking blacksmiths who could manufacture weapons for our movement. Most peasants were expected to own a helmet of leather or iron, plus a long knife, axe or spear, but I wanted a supply of heads for war scythes, poleaxes, spears and halberds – stabbing, pulling and cutting weapons. The iron heads could easily be converted to versatile polearms by attaching them to a long shaft which any peasant could supply. Happily, the local ironstone made fine metal and the forests of the Weald provided the charcoal for smelters to work it.

To properly understand the processes and ensure we had the weapons we wanted, I visited several smithies to learn their techniques. At the first, not far from our mill at Sittingbourne, a master smith called Piers Heakin showed me the process. 'We dig a mine pit to the depth of six tall men and as wide as six paces and take out the ore, using a winch to bring up a basket suspended from a tripod. The ore is that ochre-coloured stone there.' He pointed to a spoil heap that was being sifted by labourers who removed the stone and heaped it on one side. The unwanted spoil was dumped in a worked-out pit and a cartload of ore was taken to a smelting site.

'We take the ore to the charcoal because bringing the charcoal here in a cart would jolt it about and crumble it to dust,' said Master Heakin. The charcoal was created by heaping wood inside a sort of tent of cut turfs, lighting the fuel and sealing any smoking outlets to create a low-oxygen environment. This cooking removes water and other elements from the wood and produces charcoal that burns at very high temperatures with only a little smoke.

'When we have charcoal,' said Heakin, 'and oak is the best wood for it, we use it to fuel a bloomery, a sort of oven that smelts but does not melt the ore, so it doesn't absorb carbon. The treatment yields a sponge-like mass of globs of metal mingled with slag that is almost liquid. That sponge is called a 'bloom' and contains a network of channels filled with molten glass that came from impurities in the ore. The smith reheats it over and over in his furnace and hammers it – each hammer strike generates more heat – to eliminate most of the slag and create wrought iron.'

The master smith paused to scratch his nose. 'That iron is fine for some uses, as it is malleable when it's heated, but for weapons, you need to turn it into something tougher: into steel. You do that by adding a small amount of carbon to the iron, making a very tough metal which you can temper so that it is both very hard and yet a little elastic, not at all brittle.'

I looked around the smith's sooty forge where this magic took place. There was a furnace and a hearth where the iron was heated before shaping; a heavy block of iron called an anvil where the hammering took place; a leather-lunged bellows to force oxygen into the coals and boost the heat; an assortment of tongs and shaping hammers; a block with grooved sides where the work was 'swaged' or shaped; creasers, fullers, punches and drifts; chisels, tongs, augers and bits and an array of other, mysterious specialist tools.

'Can you see to work?' I asked. 'It's very gloomy in here.'

'That helps me accurately see the colour of the metal I'm working,' said Heakin. 'The temperature shows in the colour: red hot or white hot, there's a difference. Red that's visible in the dark isn't as hot as red visible in sunlight; then there's reds that are dark, dull, cherry or bright cherry. There's orange, orange-yellow, white, brilliant white and dazzling bluish white that is the hottest of all, four times hotter than the coolest red. The same goes when you're tempering, and those colours range from very pale yellow through spotted red brown to brown-yellow, full purple and very dark blue with a dozen variants in between.'

'So' – he continued the lesson –' when you've hammered out the glass from the bloom of iron, you shape it into rods. To make a sword, I take five of those rods and twist them into one blade, fusing them together by heating, folding and hammering them flat. The pounding friction of the hammer super-heats the metal and makes a powerful weld, while the mixed metals and carbon create a distinct swirling pattern down the length of the sword. I like to grind a groove down both faces of the blade. It lightens and strengthens the steel and allows you more easily to break the suction when the sword is thrust into an opponent's clinging flesh.'

Preparation finished, the smith pointed to a bubbling vat on the hearth and to a deep bucket of oil alongside.

'Tempering a sword by dunking it into boiling salts and then into oil is vital: it allows the steel to cool evenly so the blade does not fracture or warp. You don't want a brittle weapon; you want one that will hold its edge but will flex a little. Another way to achieve that is to use layered clay to coat the blade, except for the edges, before reheating it. The clay slows the cooling and makes the steel slightly softer, increasing flexibility, while the unprotected edge stays hard. A good blade bends under pressure; a poor one is brittle and snaps.

'The old Romans knew that and made sure their weapons were made with good steel. They say that when the Romans battled the Celts, who only had iron weapons, their opponents could swing their swords just two or three times before they had to step on the blades to straighten them.'

Heakin straightened up and rubbed his fire-scarred hands. 'Of course, it's more expensive to produce steel, so for implements like axes or chisels, I'll sometimes forge-weld small pieces of steel into an iron tool to give it the hardened cutting edge that's wanted.'

My tutorial ended, I stepped out into the sunlight with the smith to discuss quantities of spearheads and the like that Heakin would make for us. I handed over some gold and came away satisfied that in a couple of months we would have enough weapon heads from Heakin and his fellow smiths to arm a good fraction of our peasant army. I did not really expect a pitched battle with the king's men. I just wanted to provide a suitably martial presence and an overwhelming number of men when we confronted the nobles and their sergeants and reeves. That should cause them to reconsider actual fighting and would put us in a better position to parley with them and make our demands.

Next, I mentally turned to another problem: making sure we could keep our mob-army together after they were mustered. For shelter, most would bring something: a heavy cloak, waxed-wool cape or blanket, even a woven-straw tent; as countrymen, they would know about sleeping rough and I was not so concerned about their ability to make themselves comfortable on a gentle May night in England.

Feeding the army I envisioned we would gather was another matter. For the most part, I anticipated that each peasant would bring food of his own, but it would be wise to have at least some emergency supplies, as careless men would eat all their provisions at once and would either steal more or abandon the campaign to return home. It was best to control matters; therefore, I made a point on my travels to contact bakers and dairymen. From the former, I ordered sacks of flour and told them to be ready to create a supply of twice-baked bread at short notice. Next, I put a dozen dairymen on similar notice to make hard cheeses that could stay edible for a month or more. I also contacted brewers and orchardmen to brew barrels of small beer and prepare sacks of fruit, all of it to be delivered at a time and to a rendezvous I would specify later. The fortune I'd won in France made a powerful persuader: I could hand over gold coins in advance with the promise of more against the day our peasant army would go on the march. We would be in well-watered, rich lands so that, if we really needed to, we could buy sheep or cattle anywhere and cook them where we camped.

Transport of our stores and spares might be a problem, but we did have gold, so we could hire the peasants' own carts if needed and, as we did not plan to go great distances – I envisioned Lincoln or Oxford as the extent of our travels – the men could walk that far. I did not expect to be fighting battles, only to have confrontations that, because of the size I expected our force to be, would intimidate the nobles we might face into settling for parleys.

What caused us most concern was a surge in the pestilence and hearing of some alarming symptoms that were new to us: plague victims who did a brutal dance of death they were unable to stop.

John Wrawe, a sober, serious prelate, told our brotherhood's gathering of witnessing the macabre caperings of a goodwife in Broadstairs. 'She was in the marketplace where merchants were setting out their stalls when she began to dance. People stood staring at her, but she would not, could not stop. She whirled and gambolled, unceasing, right through the day and into the night. Her husband tried to stop her but she wept and groaned – she continued to cavort until around midnight when she collapsed on the cobbles. I heard she was up and dancing again after an hour or so and not shame, not exhaustion, not even the pain of bloodied feet could stop her hopping and whirling about.

'She danced in silence to the rhythm of unseen music, only her heart keeping tempo as she plunged and leaped to stay in motion. Two physicians came to help her but she could not stop despite their pleas and attempts to force her to be still. She danced on through two more days and nights, then died there on the street, having gyrated herself to fatal exhaustion.'

Wrawe said he had heard of other cases in Strasbourg, where dancers had been taken for prayer sessions at the shrine of St Vitus, whose feast day is celebrated by dancing before his statue, but they, too, had worked themselves to death. 'They did not exhibit the buboes and blood of the Great Pestilence, but they had caught something that possessed their minds,' he said, 'and I fear it will be coming to England.'

Certainly, the pestilence was back, and in force, so when I chose to ride to Lincoln to spread word of our uprising plans, I opted to wear a leather mask across my nose and mouth, the whole thing soaked in vinegar. It made a stink and it half-pickled the flesh of my cheeks, but the moderate sting was merely something to endure and a small price to pay to avoid the disease we were warned was rampaging.

I needed a horse so I found a stable and bought a fine chestnut stallion from a horse coper. I examined the beast closely, sure it must have been stolen, for the price he asked was small. It is easy to disguise a horse, especially if it is kept with many others. It can be given an enema so that its head will droop listlessly; it can be clipped and rubbed with oak gall to darken the coat; its mane and tail can be cut, braided or shaped differently; there are a score of means to disguise a stolen animal. I looked for all this but the animal seemed an honest sale.

The trader watched me examine the beast, then said: 'He's not stolen, lord. There are a lot of fine mounts for sale – people die, people flee. Beasts are plentiful now.' I accepted the explanation, bought a good, solid saddle tree to distribute my weight on the stallion's back, filled my saddle bags with dried meat and hard-baked bread and set out on the Great North Road.

Chapter 22

Resistance

The journey was long, even though I travelled from dawn until almost dusk, and it was ominous. I passed by village after empty village, the silence broken only by the lowing of desperate, byre-trapped cattle complaining to be milked. I soon chose to avoid riding through the villages themselves, preferring to pass by them in fields, for often, shrouded, putrid bodies lay in village streets awaiting the death carts. Sometimes I would pass an open pit where lime-doused corpses lay unburied in heaped confusion, evidence of how they had been unceremoniously tossed in, often without a single soul to mourn them because the entire family had died.

Some few times, outside the villages, I came across the unburied corpse of a human; spot-blackened and bloody, with great boils oozing pestilence into the air. I would cautiously touch my vinegar-soaked mask closer to my mouth and nose and urge my steed on past, through the silence of untended orchards, fields and gardens where animals roamed among the abandoned crops. Several times, I came across nuns and priests who were among the few to care for the sick, but they, too, would succumb to the infections that swept their convents and abbeys. In fact, most closed communities like prisons, barracks, ghettos or castles were soon swept clean of life by the latest, swamping wave of pestilence.

Occasionally I would see other travellers, usually in a small family group but we skirted each other, as we avoided the hamlets where armed men waved us away with threats. Once, I saw a place where villagers had set up baskets and coins a few hundred yards away from the hamlet's limits, asking travellers to leave food in exchange for money. At the River Nene, which I crossed on a sturdy wooden bridge, I was halted by armed men and a plague doctor hired by a town guild. The physician stepped forward, waving the guards back. He was eager to question me; where I had travelled, what I had seen? I told him what I could, which was what he mostly knew already.

That knowledge led him to protect himself against the pestilence by wearing heavy clothes, gauntlets and a wide-brimmed hat. He guarded his nose and mouth behind a posy of flowers through which he inhaled and he carried a longish stick to use in examinations of his patients so he could avoid contact and lessen the chance of contracting the plague himself. 'The plague follows a certain pattern,' he told me, his voice muffled through his posy. 'A fever comes, with vomiting of blood, sneezing, coughing and great sweating. The patient complains of weakness, of aches and chills. Often the tongue is coated white; great red and black boils the size of hen's eggs appear on the body, especially in armpits and groin and throat. The end is close then, and the patient pisses black urine and stinks foully.

'For some, death takes only hours; for others, four days of blistering torment is their lot, with a madman's writhing dance of death in pain at the finish.' I nodded. I'd heard that from John Wrawe. The physician, who probably would contract the plague himself in short order, warned of depraved people who, infected with the pestilence, would threaten to contaminate those who had locked themselves away. 'The Lord will understand if you defend yourself against such sinners,' he warned. 'Do not be afraid to use your sword.'

From him, I learned that the church, in desperation, had authorised even laymen to hear another's confession so the faithful could die shriven. The doctor also laid out what town burgesses had ordained as measures against the pestilence, again ordering the infected to stay indoors, to mark the doors of the houses of plague victims and to shut them up for at least five weeks. Their bedding and clothes should be burned, and the dead buried only in the calmer air after nightfall and at a place designated just for victims of the Great Malady.

The living, he told me, should burn juniper or rosemary, sage, bay or frankincense to cleanse the air in their houses and should heat stones of flint in the fire, then drop them into buckets of vinegar to give off purifying steam. Floors, tables and food preparation surfaces should be scrubbed with a solution of mint, pennyroyal and vinegar. Butter, the plague doctor told me, was a good preventive against the pestilence. A brew called Plague Water strengthened the body's resistance, too.

It was composed of distilled wine and an assortment of roots, leaves and herbs including chamomile, linseed, rose leaves, angelica, wormwood, rue, peony and wheat. 'Drink such draughts,' he told me earnestly, 'and you may be spared. There are no reports of the pestilence north of here, so you may well be safe in Lincoln. See a confessor, though; it is best to be prepared.'

Cautiously, I asked him about the Lollards and probed to see if he had wind of any uprising against our feudal masters. To my surprise, he nodded vigorous agreement. 'About time we got these people off our necks,' he said briskly. 'We've had several preachers through here in recent months: Wycliffe of York and the curate Wrawe as well as some of the so-called Poor Preachers. They had some common sense things to say but they'll have to look out for their necks. Our great lords would hang them for sedition.'

'Are you not putting yourself at risk with this talk?' I asked quietly.

He shrugged. 'I'll be lucky to last another month with this pestilence about. What should I fear?'

I left that brave man with his self-imposed duty of tending the dangerous infected and went on to Lincoln to meet some fellow conspirators. Several of them were in the wool trade and had much to say about troubles in Flanders which had vastly reduced trade and seriously diminished revenue from English customs taxes. 'The exchequer is about drained,' boomed one wealthy merchant who was whispered to have close connections with the throne. 'My Lord the Earl of Buckingham is squandering what little is left in the royal coffers with his expensive and unnecessary military ventures against France. Worse, Parliament is considering even more crippling taxes to be levied on the common man, despite the crop failures and the number of people who are near starving. They have already issued writs for Parliament to consider what taxes to levy but feel that the angry mob make it too dangerous to meet in London, so they have sneaked off to Northampton to hold their Parliament in safety.'

So drained was the royal treasury, he told me, that Archbishop Sudbury, chancellor of the exchequer, had pledged the king's jewels against a loan that was coming due quite soon. 'The garrisons in Brest, Cherbourg and Calais have not been paid for three months now and Sudbury says he needs the outrageous sum of £160,000 to get the king's coffers on an even keel.'

A florid-faced grandee in a purple velvet cap seemed as connected as the wealthy merchant. 'Sudbury should keep to praying. He's no politician,' he boomed. 'All the treasure the chancellery has poured out to sustain this war with France has been wasted and that gold has been thrown away just as the revenues have shrunk beyond belief. He might be an honest man but he's a fool and he's been borrowing from everyone. It's humiliating enough that the crown jewels of England may soon be in the hands of some Jewish moneylender, but at the rate Sudbury is squandering money he'll have the shirts off our backs, too.'

In a few days, news came that Parliament had chosen a route to extricate the nation from its debts. 'The Commons think that workmen and labourers who are in great demand and are being well paid since the Great Pestilence now have the money, so they've decided they should mostly bear the burden of a poll tax,' said Purple Cap. 'Of course, this lets the Commons out, and they voted that the peasants should cough up £100,000. They neatly kept themselves more or less clear by also voting that, as the church holds about one-third of the land in this kingdom, they should shoulder some responsibility and should hand over the other £60,000. It's an unfair but tricky way to dodge paying anything much themselves. It's so bad that the treasurer, the Bishop of Exeter, has saved his own scrawny neck by resigning and washing his hands of the whole business.'

Exeter's Bishop Brantingham displayed a clear understanding of what might happen and took steps to avoid it by resigning. The unfortunate who replaced him as treasurer was Sir Robert Hales, the Prior of the Knights Hospitallers and his acceptance of the role would one day bring him great unpopularity and a brutal death. But that was in the future. For now, the people had to deal with a situation that called for a shilling per head for each adult person (aged over fifteen years) in a village or township. This, explained Purple Cap, was a reasonable levy in a place where a great landowner happened to live, because the wealthy household paid many groats and the labourer paid only a few pence.

In a poor village, however, all paid the full shilling because there was no moneyed resident to subsidise the tax. The result, I soon discovered, was that most poor villages made false returns to the serjeants and constables whose duty it was to assess the population and collect the tax. Those officials either turned a blind eye to the undercount or were forced by their neighbours into accepting that England's population had almost halved in the past four years. The peasants had hidden the existence of the unmarried females in their households, suppressing reports of widowed mothers and aunts, sisters and young daughters despite the fact that in established farming communities there are usually more females than males.

When the figures came in, the government was not deceived. They compared the one-groat poll tax figures from 1377 with the new and unlikely poll count that seemed to depopulate villages because the locals did not wish to admit to having residents for whom they must pay. One of the king's serjeants at arms, John Legge, declared that the constables and collectors of the new tax had behaved with shameless corruption and negligence. Just a few weeks of investigations in Norfolk and Suffolk revealed that peasants there had suppressed the names of more than 20,000 tax-evaders. Legge sent a new force of commissioners to travel across the country to compel payment from those who had dodged the levy and to imprison any who resisted.

The preacher John Wrawe gave us the news at a churchyard gathering where we were preparing to protest at Westminster over this unfair and monstrously heavy tax. 'The king's men discovered the fraud because it was too widespread and too unbelievable, but what they plan to do is even more unbelievable. They think they can punish and imprison tens of thousands of honest Englishmen for resisting an unfair tax and they are sending out commissioners with just a half-dozen clerks each to investigate and make arrests. They are not even sending armed men to back up their extortionists!'

Suddenly, all our grumbling and planning crystallised. We could resist, and so we would.

Chapter 23

Falconer

Wat Tyler called the meeting and as it was pouring down during a February rainstorm we held it discreetly, not in a busy place like Maidstone or Canterbury, but in the rural setting of the tithe barn of St Michael's church in Bowerfield. The village was once my home; the vicar was an ally and, coincidentally, the barn was just a few hundred paces from where my wives Lizzie and Alice and the latter's stillborn baby girl lay buried near the altar. Although I am not religious, I went first to the church to mutter a prayer for the slim, bright girls who had brought us such joy and I confess that a tear or two leaked from my eyes. But I was not there on pilgrimage. This was to be a war council and I steeled myself to focus as I left the small church and made my way to the tithe barn.

The preachers John Wrawe and John Wycliffe were present but their ordained colleague John Ball was not because he was again in prison at the orders of Archbishop Simon Sudbury. My cousins Jude and Henry were in attendance with me, as was the leech collector, our 'invisible messenger' Owen Blackburn. Oliver the falconer joined us in the barn and Robert Roberts, the Gwent archer who had been a mercenary at Caffa. Piers Heakin and several other blacksmiths also arrived together. I also saw a fellow called Hornbrook whom I had heard was a coiner and I resolved to speak with him privately about my supply of silver and gold. The artisans and traders were well represented. I spotted a saddler, a devious mealman who dealt in gritty flour, a spicer, a fuller, three miners and a mason among the forty or so peasants. Some of them were more attracted by the novelty of seeing a former slave of the Mongols than of planning a campaign.

Richard Whittington of Gloucester, a fine-feathered bird in our rustics' gathering, attracted many eyes, for he was Master of the Mercers' Company and a wealthy man. A dozen or so Lollards who followed Wycliffe clustered quietly together as did a ragged group of hedge-priests who called themselves the Poor Preachers. The person who drew most attention, however, was Christian Bowdon, the boy captured by the Mongols and enslaved by them for years.

He carried on his cheek a tattoo of an H with a small circle above and explained that his captors had inscribed it, saying it was a Christian emblem which they had adapted to their own religion because it pointed to the four compass points of the world and was appropriate, as he had been a sailor in his master's fleet. He carried another tattoo on his forearm of what looked like an exploding fire lance that was shooting out an arrow or bolt and a few bullets, and he had a third more elaborate tattoo on his bicep that showed a diving peregrine.

Asked about the markings, he explained that one was Fujian fireworks that were once used for entertainment, but that some warrior khan had created a hollow tube and employed the explosive material to shoot out both a short spear like the quarrel from a crossbow and simultaneously eject a number of lead bullets. 'I have a formula to make the explosive powder,' he said. 'It used to be carefully guarded, like the possession of silkworms, but they said that in recent years the khans are much less secretive about it.'

The information about a new weapon was interesting, as was his casual mention that he had been a falconer to his Mongol master – hence the tattoo – but Christian's real value was in being able to tell us just how the Fujians had organised their uprising against their Mongol lords. 'They explained matters to their supporters, demonstrated how the system was failing them and not only told how it should be, but laid out a clear plan of how to achieve that end.'

We listened in rapt silence as he said: 'You'll need to create a way forward that all understand and assign specific duties to each person according to what skills they possess. Do not jealously keep leadership roles to just a few people: the more diverse skills and viewpoints the better, so long as you do not allow debates to grow into stubborn arguments. Try to gain insights into your opponents' thinking – people who are inside your enemy's orbit can provide much that is useful, especially if they can identify areas of weakness. You must also identify who or what brings strengths to your opponent, then ruthlessly eliminate them. Remember that if you fail in an uprising, you will lose your head. It is better that your enemy loses his, first.'

Christian looked around the circle of ragged people sitting on hay bales, standing or squatting on the dusty floor of the barn. 'We should take note of the portents and signs God sends us: signals that approve the righteousness of what we are doing. Stars that fall from the sky, floods, drought, crop failures and years of pestilence are signs that God does not support the present system – he is dismayed by it.'

John Wrawe interrupted: 'You might feel that justifies rebellion against the boy who wears the crown. In fact, the uprising is not against the king: he is a child. It is his corrupt regents and ministers that we want unseated.'

'Pray for our young King Richard,' Christian agreed, 'and revolt against those who mislead him and tread you down! All that we want is justice for the common people who feed the nation. You deserve not to be treated as I was, as a slave; you did not choose to be chained to a few rows of tilth to ensure that your manor lord lives a life of ease. It was an accident of birth that brought you to that and you deserve the right to leave it for a better life. If the lord will not grant you that right, then take it for yourself!'

Christian stopped speaking, dusted his palms against his sides and looked around. A dead silence followed his speech. Then, like a thunderclap, a burst of cheering erupted, scattering a pair of pigeons that were roosting in the hammerbeam rafters. We had a leader who seemed able to inspire our rustic legion.

The meeting broke up but few wanted to leave in the pouring rain so we stood around in the barn, talking, and the former chaplain John Wrawe sought out Christian. 'I am very interested to hear more about this explosive powder you came across in the East. It was written about by the Franciscan friar Roger Bacon some years ago. He credited its invention to the Tang dynasty several hundred years ago. He called it black powder and published a formula for making it.'

Christian nodded. 'I also have a formula,' he said. 'Essentially, it mixes charcoal, sulphur and saltpetre and can propel a missile without bursting the tube from which the missile is fired. The Chinese also used it to shatter rock or to make tunnels. It makes unstoppable bombs and very good fire arrows.'

Wrawe was listening intently. 'Fire arrows and broken walls, eh?'

he said. 'Those might be useful should we come up against troops and fortifications.'

Christian nodded agreement. 'Such have been used to sink ships. Fire arrows work very well against wooden hulls.' Wrawe smiled thinly.

'We shall have to make some experiments, you and I,' he said. 'The nobles must not be the only ones with armaments.'

'Indeed, they must not,' said Richard Whittington, who had strolled across the barn to join us. 'They have enough advantage as it is. We should discover what soldiery they have and where it is stationed. We could use some eyes and ears in the royal household.'

'I wonder,' said Wrawe, staring at Christian's bicep tattoo, 'if the king needs a falconer?'

Whittington, a man of quick wit, followed Wrawe's gaze, spotted the stooping peregrine and said quickly: 'The king is a little young for that but my lord the Duke of Lancaster is fond of hawking and surely can afford a skilled servant?'

And so it was, a month later, we had a spy working in the mews of John of Gaunt, the richest man in England. Christian Bowdon, former slave of the savage Mongols, had become a liveried falconer to a royal prince. Within a matter of days, the duke himself entered the mews to visit his raptors and was in conversation with his most exotic falconer. 'Tell me of the Chinese and of the Mongols and how they wage war,' demanded the man who was the principal military commander of the throne since his older brother, the brilliant campaigner Prince Edward of Woodstock had died.

'I can't tell you much, my lord,' said Christian. 'They use a lot of horses and they have many archers but my military experience was at the siege of Caffa, and they used not much of either, there.'

The duke frowned. 'Well, you come to me as a falconer. What about the Mongols and their hawks?'

Christian smiled. 'Those birds caused a rebellion, lord. The Mongols demanded that the Chinese supply them with gyrfalcons, which only a king may fly under our English Laws of Ownership and the Chinese resented it—'

'Yes, yes, I know all about that,' said the duke, who rather regretted moving up from the fast-stooping peregrine he'd been so proud of when he was an earl. Now, as a duke, he was entitled to fly a slower merlin, though that predator was faster in level flight. 'Tell me the Mongols' training secrets.'

Christian took a breath. 'Well, there's hawks and there's falcons. Hawks are bigger birds and count eagles and vultures in their group. They chase, then pounce on their prey and kill with their talons. Falcons, on the other hand, don't chase: they dive onto their prey at speed, crash in with their talons then break their target's neck, using a notch in their beaks to sever the spine.

'I catch them young and get them used to humans. "Manning" we call it. If you carefully sew their eyelids shut, they have to pay attention to you, and they're certainly not inclined to fly away. I take her with me, hood her and put her on a perch by my bed so she knows my scent and my voice. In time, I remove the stitches and she can see, but by then she'll know me and come to me. I feed them on the fist and, when she is flying, she soon learns that when she comes back to my fist, she gets attention and food. She sees so well; you'd find it hard to believe. Her eyes clear and refocus two or three times faster than a man's even when she's diving at high speed and a falcon's side vision is absolutely clear so she can see about eight times better than a human.'

He moved a small leather pouch slung on his belt and showed the duke a bloody lump of meat and feathers. 'Quail,' he said briefly. 'The falcon needs more than meat alone; she needs roughage to clean her crop. She then spits out a round grey pellet called a casting.' Christian stopped talking as a boy approached. 'Ah, good, my lord,' he said. 'Here's the cadger.' Lancaster was intrigued despite himself. He knew little about training the hunting birds and his other falconers, awed by his intimidating presence, had never offered instruction in case he disagreed with it.

Owning hunting birds was an expensive business; stealing one was punishable by death. Even for a peasant to own one, unlikely as it was that he could afford to do so, could put him at risk of punishment for having a raptor of a standing above his station.

The boy approached the falconer and the duke nervously. On his back he was wearing a 'cadge', a wooden rack on which two birds sat quietly under their soft red leather hoods. Christian, moving with easy, slow motions, unfastened the leather jesses which held one bird, a peregrine, to the cadge and slipped a long length of twine onto her leg. 'The creance,' he said, fastening the long tether that allowed him to control the bird while he exercised and trained her. 'I "reclaim" her by pulling in the tether,' he said, beginning to knot the jesses that hung from the bird's legs and looping them around his little finger. 'She's a longwing, and you need to control her properly. Now I have her literally wrapped around my finger.'

Christian flicked the two tiny silver bells on her legs and touched the silver swivel bands called tyrrits that fitted over his fingers and secured the bird. A last look at the tethers, thongs and rings to see all was in place and he gently slipped the leather hood from the bird's head and proffered his upraised forefinger under its stout leather gauntlet. The peregrine promptly hopped onto it, seeking the highest perch. The falconer clamped down on her talons. 'Now, I have her under my thumb.'

Lancaster stood frankly admiring the peregrine, a handsome, blue-barred killer that was queen of the skies and she turned her bright, intelligent eyes on him. 'She's the fastest bird in the world when she dives on her prey,' said Christian proudly. 'It's called a stoop when she folds her wings and plunges out of the sky. Only an eagle or a gyrfalcon could challenge her, but you know, they're bigger birds that can knock down geese or herons. This peregrine can take down ducks, bats, songbirds and she's so fast she can hit them, kill them and catch them in midair. She's intelligent, loyal – she mates for life – and she is a fierce defender of her chicks and her territory. She's the best of the raptors.'

Lancaster, a grandee used to dominating the conversation, interjected: 'What about the saker falcon? A lot of my knights hunt with them.'

Christian hesitated, aware of his humble standing and of this Plantagenet's royal temper. 'Yes, he is a big and powerful bird, lord, but he has blunt wings and he's not as fast. He's better than the lanner, though. That red-headed fellow is just for squires' use.'

I sensed that the duke was irritated at being corrected, so hastily asked about the other bird perched on the cadge.

'Oh, yes,' said Christian, 'he's a kestrel, a windhover. Some call him a sparrow hawk, a child's hunting bird, but he's a gallant little fellow and what a flier! He can hang absolutely motionless in the air as he searches for prey. I've seen one inside a tithe barn, just hovering, looking for mice, and when he spotted one, he was down like a stone, straight onto it.'

The peregrine began to stir and started beating her wings. 'She's hot,' said Christian confidently. 'She's bating. I'll sort her out.' He hooded the bird and, with her still flapping on his wrist, walked to the mews door. Under the eave outside was a granite horse trough, its water green with slime. Christian lowered a wooden dipper into it and poured the contents over the bird's back and hood, soaking and cooling her. The agitated bating stopped at once.

The falconer settled the bird on a rail of the cadge, looping her jesses around it to keep her tethered. He slipped off the hood and began feeding her pieces of the quail he had in his pouch, using his fingers, which were gauntleted for protection from the bird's fierce beak. 'She's a good bird, lord,' he said. 'She'll do well for you in the hunt.'

Lancaster grunted. 'Make sure she does,' he said curtly, and strode away.

Christian turned to me and said quietly: 'It's going to be a pleasure to teach a lesson to that arrogant son of a Flemish butcher. We'll see how he feels when the peasants have taught him some manners.'

Chapter 24

Joan

My lord the Duke of Lancaster was certainly high-handed, as could almost be expected from one of his standing. He was the third son of the old king Edward and had claims to the thrones of Castile and Léon by right of marriage – he even styled himself as King of Castile. He was arguably the richest man in England, thanks to some highly advantageous unions and having been handed some generous land grants. He held great castles at Kenilworth, Queenborough and Hertford and spent a fortune improving the fortress of Windsor. He was uncle to our boy king Richard and, after the deaths of his older brother Edward of Woodstock and their father King Edward, had taken over many of the functions of government. For all practical purposes he was the regent ruler, acting as a surrogate king in place of his nephew, who was just ten years old when he came to the throne. We all remembered the day; it was a great day of public celebration and a grand parade through the streets of London.

I was at Westminster to see the boy king arrive at a fake castle made to look like the New Jerusalem. Actors dressed as heavenly angels crowned him to show that he was God's Chosen and, like every boy in England, I had obeyed the law and sworn an oath of lifelong loyalty to King Richard and to all his descendants.

The parade was not the only one seen at the royal court. Richard's uncle, John of Gaunt, Duke of Lancaster, lived in great state and, as the boy's closest adult male relative, took decisions and acted for him. 'He acts as a king and even travels like one,' John Wrawe once said after seeing the train of 150 men-at-arms and 115 servants who accompanied the duke on a royal progress.

For all his wealth and power, Gaunt was not popular with the common people and even his role as one of England's most important military commanders was outshone by the actions of his older brother, Edward of Woodstock, the Black Prince. Like Edward, Lancaster had led mounted raids across France, but his incompetence was evident, and his few successes were pallid by comparison to those of the prince, one of the greatest warriors of his age. Although his personal courage was unquestioned, Lancaster had faced but not fought the French for three weeks of standoff. He had advocated a truce and peace, which angered the common folk who wanted to see more triumphs like those we English had won at Crecy and Poitiers. They howled for Lancaster's blood when French pirates sacked Plymouth, Portsmouth and Rye; they were outraged that England, whom the Black Prince had led to triumph after triumph in France, was threatened on the Scottish border, at Bordeaux and at Calais, our most important foothold in France.

When he tried to relieve our beset holdings in Aquitaine, Gaunt led a winter raid across France but was plagued by disease and starvation, battered by the French and weakened so badly he lost two-thirds of the original 9,000 men who had set out from Calais. With his force mutinous and unpaid, he abandoned the campaign and sailed home.

'John of Gaunt? People don't trust him,' said Wrawe. 'He only wants a truce with France to release soldiers so he can use them himself, raise an army and enforce his claim to Castile. Worse, he's having an affair with the old king's corrupt whore, Alice, who's robbing the exchequer blind. I think he plans to take over the throne by stealing it from his nephew although he pays lip service to sustaining the boy as king. He's a snake!'

After meeting the man, I felt there was truth in Wrawe's assessment but I had other, more urgent things on my mind. I had to distribute the weapons the smiths were making and I needed secretly to gather and store food and drink for our planned army. Both weapons and supplies needed some secure hiding places that were also discreet. I thought I had the answer. I would approach Joan of Kent, the boy king's mother. Countess Joan, known to history as the Fair Maid of Kent was a baroness, Lady of the Garter and England's most famous beauty. She was a Plantagenet, a granddaughter of King Edward Longshanks and daughter of his son, Edmund, Earl of Kent, who had been executed after attempting to overthrow the usurper Roger Mortimer, leaving Joan to be brought up by her widowed mother. At age thirteen, the girl secretly married the Lancashire knight Thomas Holland, an adventurer and freebooter who, soon after their union, left for the wars in France to serve with the Black Prince and my old friend Robert Knollys.

Holland returned from campaigning to find that her mother had married off Joan to the Earl of Salisbury. The girl later explained that she kept her first marriage secret because she was afraid it could lead to Holland's execution for treason, as she was the king's ward and needed his permission to marry, which the couple had failed to seek. Holland petitioned the Pope in Avignon and presented him with a suitable gift – a relic claimed to be a feather from the Angel Gabriel's wing – to earn them an annulment of Joan's second 'marriage' and a papal blessing on their secret union, which was a fruitful and happy union.

At Holland's death, his friend, the Black Prince, married Joan and the royal couple had five offspring before the prince's untimely death. Their first son, heir to the English throne, also died and their second son, Richard of Bordeaux was only ten years old when he succeeded his grandfather as king, so his uncle John of Gaunt, Duke of Lancaster assumed the duties of ruler until Richard was older. Although Gaunt was unpopular with the common people, Joan was beloved as a gentle, charitable soul and I felt she would sympathise with the peasantry who wanted to end the old system of tithes and labour services.

Also, as a royal princess, she had properties where food and military supplies could be quietly and safely stored. Better still, she had a known sympathy for the Lollards, that religious reform movement led by the Oxford scholar and priest John Wycliffe. I went to see him when he was preaching in Maidstone and I took the wealthy mercer Richard Whittington with me. We quickly outlined the situation to Wycliffe: we were readying to present our demands to the king and his counsellors once we had organised and equipped our various groups in Kent, Suffolk and Essex. We could use Joan's help in several ways, chiefly to influence her son to approve our wishes and, also, to use some of her properties to store our supplies safely and secretly. We wanted no word of our preparations to leak out; we wanted to surprise the nobles and the church with our numbers, our readiness and our determination to act.

With our goals agreed, we travelled up the Thames in a stout barge to Wallingford, Berkshire, where Joan was in residence at the riverside castle and had agreed to meet us. We strode into the courtyard, past some bemused guards and were led by a tipstaff to the solarium where the countess was chatting with one of her maids. She nodded the girl permission to slip away and turned to greet us, gesturing for us to draw seats to a long table as she seated herself opposite us. I have to say that my first sight of Joan stunned me. She was not young but I had never seen such a beautiful woman and I drank in her appearance even before she sat. I gulped and told myself: 'Tom Thatcher, this is how angels must look.'

The Dowager Princess of Wales, Joan, was a woman in her mid-years, of medium height, slender and graceful. She had auburn hair lit with strands of grey and wide grey-green eyes with long, light-coloured lashes. Her complexion was creamy with delicate peach colouring, her skin smooth and unsullied, her nose graceful and her teeth white and even above a full lower lip. Her neck was as graceful as a swan's, above a pretty bosom, trim waist and the gentle curves of thighs beneath her kirtle. I drank in every detail down to her small feet in blue velvet slippers. Joan was rightly described by the court historian Jean Froissart as 'The most beautiful woman in all the realm of England' and I cannot disagree.

Whittington, the crafty mercer, stepped forward briskly, bowed deep, and diffidently presented the countess with a gift taken from his finest stock: a long-sleeved silk tunic brilliantly dyed with saffron made from the stamens of the crocus flower. When Joan unwrapped it, she gasped – it was a gift worth more than gold – and we knew we had won an ally. Next, I also bowed low to place a small packet on the table before the countess: 'Dried ginger, my lady,' I explained.

'Oh, that is so wonderful!' she said. 'How did you come by it?'

'It travelled from China and I brought it with me from the Black Sea, lady,' I said.

'I am so grateful,' said Joan. 'Ginger is said to ward off the pestilence but I also have tasted a drink made from it, and loved it. Thank you so very much!'

Wycliffe, the Oxford scholar, produced a more subtle gift: a Bible translated from St Jerome's vulgate Latin into English, bound in vibrant, soft red leather. He explained: 'My lady, we should put a copy of this into every church, so the common people can read of Our Lord in their own language. This will help them better to know the scriptures – which I regret that even many vicars do not.' He paused; Joan looked thoughtful, and Wycliffe smoothly continued: 'Christ honoured the common people. We have the opportunity to bring His word to each of them. This could be the enduring and invaluable Christian legacy of your son the king.'

I glanced at Whittington and he subtly nodded to me. He knew when an agreement had been reached, even before the countess knew it herself. The countess looked down at her feet, lost in thought for what seemed an age but was merely a minute or so. Finally, she looked up at us and asked directly, 'How can we make this happen?'

Wycliffe had his moves plotted ahead like a chess master. He leaned forward, concerned, serious, honest. 'Because of the king's youth, he needs be guided by you, lady, and by his counsellors. Many of the common people regard his uncle John of Gaunt as less than a perfect advisor. Indeed, they suspect he may have ambitions and plans of his own, ones that are not always in the king's best interests. Forgive me speaking so boldly, but I wish you, lady, to be clear about the real situation, not to be swayed by honeyed words that do not truly represent the matter.'

Joan was no fool and she nodded briefly.

'Be forthright with me, Master Wycliffe,' she said. 'There are often dangerous currents in the rivers of royalty and you must understand that my chief desire is to see my son well advised and in no danger.'

We all took in the hint. The countess, too, was suspicious of her late husband's younger brother and his ambitions. Wycliffe continued: 'Your husband the prince was a great man and one beloved by his people. His was a sad loss and a grievous one for England. Our ambitions include helping you and your son the king to put the nation back on its tracks. The common people are not eager to continue expensive wars that serve little purpose. We are still struggling with the remnants of the Great Pestilence; few households have escaped tragic losses. Why must we continue to see our people endure more sorrows fighting a war that is not for the common good?' What we left unsaid was that those who should represent humble serving men – the mayor and other elected officials of a town – re-elected themselves without regard for the rights and wishes of the majority. It was not something to put to a noble member of that governing class.

Joan was speaking: 'And how, Master Wycliffe – and you, my masters' – with a nod to Whittington and myself – 'will you persuade the king's advisors and especially the Duke of Lancaster to do as you ask?'

I saw Wycliffe's knuckles whiten as he gripped the arms of his chair. This was where the countess might shout 'Treason!' and call in the guards. If Wycliffe made threats, our heads might be on pikes above the gatehouse of the White Tower. 'We will show his grace the duke that we support the king,' said Wycliffe.

I heard my own voice interject: 'We will show my lord Lancaster what he understands, in the language he knows best. We will bring an army of Englishmen to demand justice and an end to the old, abusive system. England must be made again into a good place for everyone, not be a land where a mere few benefit from the labours of the many.'

Joan looked at me and a small smile curved her lips. 'So, you have a voice, Master Thatcher. I am pleased to hear it.' I probably shuffled on my seat.

'My voice is one of many, my lady,' I said. 'I am merely a conduit for some of the peasantry of England to have their voices heard.'

Whittington alertly stepped in. 'My cousin Tom here makes no threats, Lady Joan,' he said. 'He only demonstrates the love Englishmen have for their king and promises that they will brook no diversion of your son's authority to others who do not act in his interests.' With that, an invisible sword was drawn, and its unspoken threat lay on the table between us.

Wycliffe spoke again in a gentle voice. 'We are offering you the support of Englishmen, my lady,' he said. 'We will show our teeth if we must but we will not bare them to the king or yourself. We are your servants. In fact, what we do does have legal precedents. Burgesses and barons once cited ancient custom in their struggles against unpopular kings, and so too can those who hold land as villeins claim exemptions that are laid out in the Domesday Book.'

I'd heard the argument when some hedge-lawyer spouted it at a village gathering. Now, when Wycliffe noted it, I listened. He argued that the tax records gathered after the Normans came – the Domesday Book that two centuries before had listed every holding, beast and manor in England – specified that if the baron who ruled them did not apply proper codes of conduct, then the serfs were discharged of their manorial duties and had the right to 'constrain their lords by the strong hand'. This, said Wycliffe, was exactly what we were now doing: since the pestilence there had not been enough manpower to work the land as before and villeins were being subjected to cruel decisions that prevented them from finding profitable work. 'We may be protesters but we do not go against our king,' he said. 'We merely cite the laws your royal ancestors laid down for their servants. We are against corruption and we stand for King Richard and the true commons.'

The countess looked gravely at each of us in turn, assessing us. 'I believe you are faithful servants of our king,' she said, 'and I appreciate the honesty you have brought to me today. What practical steps do you take? Can I assist?' Suddenly, we were plunged into a morass of details: how we were organising our companies and guilds, what we planned to demand, how we were readying our show of force. We emptied a pack animal's burden of minutiae into the countess' ears.

'You say you are amassing weapons, Master Thatcher?'

I nodded. 'We must convince others that we are serious and cannot be forced to continue our old roles. Some nobles only understand might, so we will demonstrate that. A thousand men with weapons are more convincing than a few humble petitioners on their knees begging to be heard. We are united in this. By God's beard we will hang together, or we will hang separately.'

Joan looked uneasy at the mention of hanging and lifted the leather-bound Bible. 'This is a remarkable colour, Master Wycliffe,' she said. 'How did you come by it?'

Wycliffe took the hint and changed direction. 'A dyer who found the leather for me explained it, my lady,' he said smoothly. 'It is called Turkey Red. It takes months to produce and uses the root of the rubia plant, olive oil and cattle products including blood.'

Later, he whispered to me that the 'cattle product' he did not name was dung. 'But she'd never take that Bible to church if she knew how it stank before being applied.'

The countess grimaced at the word 'blood' but said brightly: 'How informed you are, Master Wycliffe. Do you know any more of the dyers' secrets?'

'They are a guild, a brotherhood, my lady,' he said. 'They keep their secrets, as we keep ours, but I can tell you that the Tyrian purple trimming of your royal cloak comes from the murex sea snail, a predator that uses an excretion to subdue its prey. That excretion is the source of the fine purple colour of your cloak.'

'So,' said Joan thoughtfully, 'the dyers' guild keeps these secrets and works together?'

'As would we, my lady,' said Wycliffe.

Chapter 25

Preparations

Countess Joan was sincere when she asked what assistance she could give but even she gasped when she realised the far-flung extent of our web of collaborators. We explained that ours was no mere local uprising: Kent and Essex, London and the counties around it were hotbeds of resentment against the restrictions of their local manors, but the movement was well rooted, too, with leagues and societies in Norfolk and Suffolk, Cambridgeshire and Huntingdonshire, right across the eastern counties to the German Sea and as far north as outlying counties like Lancashire, Yorkshire and Cheshire. To protect themselves from the wrath of the landowners, these societies concealed their true purpose, declaring their meetings were for religious reasons: to carry out pious duties.

In our meeting with the countess, we did not emphasise the possible need for violence to make the barons see sense and agree to justice. Whittington and Wycliffe were no soldiers, but I had military experience and a grasp of what we would need and had recruited a core group of former soldiers – including my Thatcher cousins who had served against the Mongols – to establish dumps of stores around the shires to keep our supply lines as short as possible. Those dumps would contain at least basics for weapons – pole weapons' heads, for example – plus some equipment and some stores. Transport would be a problem – peasants generally had a shortage of draught animals – but we could commandeer carts the men could pull and our planned system of dumps could make carrying supplies relatively less difficult.

This was where Kent's princess was so valuable to us: Joan permitted us access to barns and stables, storerooms, kitchens and smithies in a dozen of her properties: places where we could safely and discreetly lodge weapons and supplies until we needed to distribute them. We knew the peasants: if we handed one of them the recently forged head of an axe or a spear to fit to a shaft, they'd soon be boastfully displaying their shiny, new weapon in a tavern or would be seen practising with it on a village green. In a day or two, sheriffs' men across the county would have had reports and would assess the usual grumblings of discontent as becoming more meaningful. Our hopes of surprising the barons would ebb away like water through sand.

If the countess, however, told her stewards to stow the grain sacks or heavy wooden boxes containing something metallic, it would be done without question, and the sacks and boxes would remain undisturbed until they were required. And that is what happened. Every so often, a farm wagon would arrive at one of the countess' manor houses; the driver would speak with the steward and a transfer would be made. Soon, we had supplies and weapons secreted across Essex and Kent, Norfolk and Suffolk, in London warehouses, in a Cheshire water mill and an Oxford college, even in a vicar's house in Lincoln. It took time but the preparations were steadily completed.

Christian was established as a falconer in Lancaster's royal household and provided connections to the noble visitors who might be sympathetic to our cause. Where we could, we made connection with them to seek funds or other assistance. We had substantial help from a former mayor of York, a Winchester draper of considerable wealth, dozens of knights and even some enlightened manorial lords. Most friars, especially the Carmelites and Dominicans, had sympathy for our cause, partly because their old doctrine of poverty for those who spread God's word underpinned John Ball's evangelism. Many friars and clerks went so far as to join our ranks and one brother became notable for leading the tenants of the monastery of Milton in Hampshire against their abbot, who had been reprimanded by the bishop for laxity.

Among the complaints investigated and found justified by His Grace was that the monks of Milton were not strict enough in their daily lives; that their bread and ale were too luxurious; that the abbot must show more kindness, must account for money which he had received but not declared, and that certain named women were no longer to be allowed access to the precincts. Also, the abbot must re-admit Brother Walter de Sherborne who had left the order to attach himself to the Brothers Preachers, an order which was more determinedly self-sacrificing, but now wished to return as he had wavered in his faith.

And, said the bishop, the drains needed to be cleaned.

Apart from grumbles about the greedy churchmen who were their landlords, the peasants generally did not have issues about religion as such. The villeins' complaints concerned taxes and levies and the manorial lords and their rapacious demands; city labourers both skilled and unskilled resented their employers; city dwellers disliked the high-handed, corrupt aldermen and mayors who failed to heed their wishes; and the dockside mobs resented foreign merchants just as workers and merchants in the wool trade hated the skilled Flemings and Zeelanders brought in by King Edward to improve their products. In the minds of uneducated peasants, all foreigners or strangers were to be treated with suspicion and even with hostility for they sweated female and child labour to undercut honest Englishmen.

'People are hurting,' Wycliffe said as we ate a bowl of pottage in a shepherd's bothy where we had begged a pallet for the night as we travelled around Kent.

'I know it,' said the shepherd bitterly. 'The weather has failed us for yet another season; floods are everywhere and the crops are almost non-existent. People are actually starving, but the local authorities still exploit the peasants. Even the young king is no help. The law that Edward laid down still stands: wages are limited by law to levels we had before the Great Pestilence, yet there are not the men to work what fields do grow. Just at a time when labourers are in demand and could command more wages, they are forbidden to travel in search of better pay.

'Because the manorial lords do not want to pay, they're making them become serfs again to save paying out money. But people aren't stupid. They know that lawyers, landowners and officials are hand in glove to keep the peasants down while they benefit.'

'And now,' he said before he scooped some more soupy beans into his mouth, 'we're getting skinned again, levied with the third poll tax in three years and it's going to crucify us worse than our Saviour suffered when He was nailed up.' Wycliffe and I nodded agreement. The man was right: the new tax was three times higher than the previous pair of imposts and, especially cruelly, it took no account of a man's ability to pay. And to what end was the tax to be used? I knew the answer, for Christian Bowdon was now feeding us invaluable information. He was eavesdropping and reporting the conversations of nobles attending his master John of Gaunt in his castle at Queenborough.

'The money is to pay for my lord Buckingham's vastly expensive, futile and failed expedition to France,' he told us. 'Chancellor Sudbury said he had pledged the king's own jewels as surety for a loan which comes due very soon and he wants £160,000 to meet the king's needs if he is to carry on the war.'

Wycliffe shook his head when I relayed Christian's message. 'That's a staggering amount. The king can't even pay his soldiers, I hear. Deserters coming through Dover say the garrisons in Calais, Brest and Cherbourg haven't been paid in months; Buckingham's men are in worse shape even than those troops and the French are raiding at will along our coasts. We need to get out of this useless war and put matters right at home.'

We could not stop the French war but we could make ready for our own confrontation. Messengers, including the Poor Preachers and the Brothers Preachers; itinerant pedlars, wandering packmen and firebrands like the Dartford baker Robert Cave all spread the word and smuggled weapons and supplies like beer, bacon, herrings and barley bread into our secret depots across the counties of the south and east. We made a list of targets: lockups in London like the Tower, the Fleet, Marshalsea, Newgate and Westminster prisons. We eyed aristocratic houses like the Savoy Palace of John of Gaunt and the grand homes and palaces of bishops as well as places where court records, property deeds and pipe rolls for Parliament and Chancery may be stored. Particular attention was paid to the fine palace occupied by Archbishop Sudbury – the chancellor who had brought such grief to us – and to a dozen or more collectors and officials who had been merciless in applying the taxes.

Our core group, the vicar John Wrawe, Lollards led by theological scholar Nicholas of Hereford, and John Litster, a Norfolk dyer who had brought a number of local knights and gentlemen to our cause, rallied around John Wycliffe the Oxford scholar and rector of Lutterworth. So, too, did the self-styled king of Suffolk, Robert Westbrom, but we missed the incendiary priest John Ball, who had been locked up again by Archbishop Sudbury.

News came to us of a London rebel, Jack Straw, whose *nom de guerre* may have resulted from his practice of delivering exhortations to crowds while standing high above them on a hay wain. Straw, we heard, was a fiery orator with an alarming habit of whipping up the crowd to demand blood. 'He wants to kill every noble and every churchman from the archbishop down,' revealed one attendee at a Straw rally. 'He says he has already made a death list.'

We, too, had lists, and we made a mistake, for the registers we created worked fatally against us. It came about like this: there was one important thing to prepare before we showed our hand. We needed a way to communicate swiftly and clearly between our scattered and disparate groups. We chose to draw up a list of men who were ringleaders in each area, men who were literate so we could communicate by written note to avoid misunderstanding or garbling of messages. The recipients of the missives should also be men regarded as leaders in their groups.

We haggled out such lists and recruited youths who could ride to deliver messages and who were familiar with the areas in which they would be carrying information and orders – although we had to be careful not to command but merely to suggest actions to men who were sometimes pridefully prickly about their new, quasi-military roles. We made a fatal error in this planning: we did not attach enough importance to guarding our lists of the leading rebels' names, a mistake that later would be paid for with a waterfall of blood.

Chapter 26

Dungeon

For several months after November 1380, when the cruel, new poll tax was announced, the peasants had eluded it. They falsely claimed that few people lived in their village; they hid from the tax collectors, who ruthlessly tried to carry out their tasks. Sometimes, to determine is a peasant was over the age of fifteen, they would insultingly demand to see a youth or maiden's privy parts, to see if he or she was past puberty. In those first weeks, the peasants felt the twin lash of humiliating powerlessness and financial loss. They not only had to pay the crippling taxes but they were also fined or imprisoned for evasion, and the resentment that had been simmering began to boil over. At the centre of this was the king's serjeant at arms, John Legge, who headed the merciless commission given the task of collecting the hated taxes.

Even some of his own men, anticipating the unpopularity that would follow, excused themselves from the duty, but Legge, either hugely courageous or massively oblivious, blundered on, accusing villagers of fraud and lies, threatening punishment and more fines and berating his listeners with the numbers he deduced had been suppressed and hidden from his commissioners. 'Hordes of you are defrauding the government: 8,000 of you in Norfolk; another 13,000 in Suffolk,' he angrily charged. 'Tens of thousands of you are thieves, cheating your king.' He challenged the mob in the marketplace at Norwich, ignoring both the ill temper and boos of the crowd and the fact that he stood virtually alone, backed only by a handful of clerks and without a single armed soldier.

Parliament slowly recognised the temper of the nation, as did the chancellor-archbishop, who had promised the House that he would not call another session to ask for money but was forced to break his word.

'There was another factor,' Wycliffe, who had spies at court and in Parliament and was among the best-informed of the malcontents, told a meeting of peasant leaders. Some of his informants were in the pay of John of Gaunt and that nobleman leaked information through them to Wycliffe because he wanted the academic and his peasant army to help him undermine the power of the church.

'There was a criminal trial going on in London,' Wycliffe continued. 'An enterprising Italian merchant who represents a syndicate in Genoa saw a chance to move the staple – a sort of clearing house for goods from the Mediterranean – from London to Southampton. The Italian planned to pay off some influential people in Parliament to grant the concession and let him quietly transfer lucrative commerce away from English traders in the capital.'

Those traders, led by an old soldier called John Kirkeby were ruthless when they discovered this challenge to their income stream. They trapped the Italian merchant, stabbed him with poisoned knives, and left his body 'like a dog's' in a stinking gutter. 'King Richard's ministers, led by Gaunt, decided to make an example of the assassins,' said Wycliffe, 'but Gaunt sniffed the wind and recognised the sympathy Londoners had for the killers and their wish to keep the wealthy trade in their own city, and chose discretion as the better part of valour. He guessed that if the merchants were found guilty, and hanged, there would be riots. In his usual high-handed way, Gaunt overrode the wishes of the king's ministers and decreed that the murder trial should be moved and held outside London, in Northampton.' Predictably, the move was seen by the peasantry as deceitful and showing fear.

At that same November parliament, out of the view and protests of the citizenry, the ministers approved the hated poll tax. The commoners grumbled that the lords who passed these laws were aristocrats and clergy, while the Commons were knights, merchants and senior gentry. 'Who represents the peasants?' the curate John Wrawe demanded at a discreet meeting in the tithe barn. 'The landowners who operate the manorial courts are not impartial. They enforce the laws to suit their wishes and act as royal judges in cases that involve themselves against their serfs!'

Our meeting dispersed into the wintry night with several groups assigned certain duties. One, led by a couple of experienced cowmen, was to locate and steal back the cattle and pigs which had been confiscated by the royal tax collectors. Others were to go to the various supplies and weapons dumps scattered across five or six counties and distribute the axe and spear heads that would make pole weapons. 'Be sure to give them out only to local captains: sober, reliable men who will not boast of owning them but will mount the weapon heads to staffs,' Tyler instructed. 'Speak with the recipients first to establish how many weapons their village will need and deliver that number to the village organiser. He can have the hedgers and ditchers who would be soldiers make the staffs for the blades, but they should not release the weapons to other peasants until we send word.'

Tyler gave similar instructions to release food supplies only to other responsible local captains who would distribute them later. That same network of captains was to encourage their 'troops' to have knives, swords, bows and helmets quietly put into good order against the time they might need to be armed. 'Caution them against loose talk in taverns: the landowners' constables have ears and we do not want to lose the advantage of surprise.'

My cousins Jude and Henry Thatcher, the red-haired shepherd Ralph Banton and the blacksmith Piers Heakin and I had a special mission: we would scout Brambles gaol in Maidstone to see if we could release John Ball. The priest was an orator who could move a mob and we could use his skills to inspire our supporters before we took up arms, but first he had to escape the archbishop's chains and bars.

I had heard Ball's sermon several times and it always echoed with the common people. It went like this: 'When Adam delved and Eve span, who was then the gentleman? From the beginning, all men by nature were created alike, and our bondage or servitude came in by the unjust oppression of evil men. For if God would have had any bondmen from the beginning, he would have appointed who should be bond, and who free. And, therefore, I exhort you to consider that now the time is come, appointed to us by God, in which you may (if you will) cast off the yoke of bondage, and recover liberty.'

Now, the priest who preached casting off bondage was himself locked away, as he had again annoyed the archbishop by preaching that a number of religious beliefs and practices were grounded not in the Bible but in dicta handed down by popes. Like Wycliffe, Ball taught that it was wrong to worship religious statues, that purgatory was a papal invention, as was pilgrimage – a lucrative source of income for the church. He taught that non-Biblical saints should not be worshipped and the doctrine of transubstantiation, that Christ's body and blood are turned into sacramental bread and wine, was also highly flawed and not sourced in any Bible teachings. I thought it likely that any of these teachings would annoy the archbishop. They did. He sent retainers out to find Ball and once again the reformist and intractable priest was imprisoned for continuing 'to preach articles contrary to the faith of the church'.

Our confraternity wanted him free and it was important to us that he be released. For over a score of years, Father Ball had wandered the countryside denouncing the way the rich exploited the poor and calling for equality and a fraternal society. He was the spiritual leader of our movement; he had access to God's word and it was important to the peasants to be led by a religious figure. Wycliffe wanted the church to change; Ball wanted the nobility to change, too. We needed Ball's rhetoric to keep our fraternity enthused.

So, we five rode to Maidstone to inspect his prison and form a plan to break him out. We soon found where he was likely to be: in a stone outbuilding south of and close to the archbishop's imposing tiled-roof palace, which is sited on the bank of the River Medway close to the confluence of the River Len. Just to the east of the Brambles gaol stands the bulk of All Saints Church. A long, hammerbeam tithe barn and stables and a sturdy half-timbered stone gatehouse comprised most of the palace compound. Across the Medway stands All Saints, a college for the training of secular priests and nearby are two hospitals built for wayfarers and pilgrims to Canterbury.

The chief building of interest to us was the Brambles dungeon, a sturdy stone edifice with two small barred windows and two entrances, one of which gave access to an ancient undercroft. After our scouting, we debated approaches. Henry and Jude suggested going through the undercroft and tunnelling up into the dungeons; Piers the blacksmith eyed the ragstone walls and iron bars and thought he could chisel through; I considered the traffic of clerics and prostitutes who visited the gaol and thought of smuggling Ball out in disguise, but Banton the shepherd came up with the simplest and probably the most effective solution: to obtain a gaoler's keys.

By a vote, that was what we opted to do. Hammering through the undercroft or removing the window bars would be too noisy; getting Ball out in the wig and dress of a whore was risky as he was well known. Capturing a gaoler to steal his keys had problems as he probably would not carry keys away from the dungeon, so the simplest way was either to overcome him at his station or to bribe him. This last, bribery to make a copy of the keys and use them when he was not on duty and could not be blamed, was most favoured; Jude argued for a drugged drink or a knock on the head, but lost the vote 4-1.

It took three days to establish the gaol routine, find where the turnkeys lived and make contact discreetly with two of them over mazers of cider in the Three Tuns tavern; so after dark we met a gaoler named Robin outside the gaol and handed over four silver coins. He slipped a key to the blacksmith Piers, who impressed it into a brick of soft clay and returned it. We vanished into the night and Piers took his clay and another silver coin to the forge of a smith he'd befriended to do a couple of hours' heating, beating, cooling and filing a piece of iron.

After that, it should have been simple. In the darkest hours of the night, Jude and I let ourselves through the door to the undercroft while Henry arrived at the riverbank in a wherry whose rower had been well paid to take him there. Ralph and Piers led our string of horses out of the stables to a quiet corner of the compound where Henry would join them after we had met him and our wherry at the river.

Jude insisted we carry weapons to our breakout of the gaoled priest and showed his knife. I was not happiest with a blade but brought a cudgel instead of my familiar quarterstaff, just in case of need, though we knew this should go as we wanted. The key worked well enough and opened an outside door to the gaol, where we found another, unlocked door at the head of a set of stone steps. Descending them cautiously, aware of the off-height sword step, we found the gaoler Robin, who got up from his stool and nodded to a heavy door across the chamber. Jude showed his key; the man motioned us forward and I began fumbling to open the dungeon door, whispering hoarsely for John Ball.

As the cell door creakily opened inwards, a burly man-at-arms stepped out and I saw two more in the gloom behind him. Jude quick-wittedly threw the gaoler's wooden stool at the fellow's knees, sending him sprawling, and I kicked him backwards. The second stepped over him but I swung a lucky cudgel blow to his temple and he stumbled, blocking the third man. I hauled the door shut. Jude menaced Robin back with the knife and pushed him to the flagstones as I turned the cell door key. Robin half rose but Jude growled that I'd smash his head into paste and he sank to his knees. We quickly chained him with a set of fetters that were hanging on a wall. The men inside the cell were kicking up noise but that was probably usual in the dungeon and no undue cause for concern, so we fled up the stairs and locked the outer door behind us to slow pursuit. We fled, but without John Ball whom we later found was not there, anyway. He had been locked up elsewhere when the treacherous cider-drinking Robin had decided to capture us as we attempted a rescue.

Fortunately, the guards had seen only two of us, so we pair raced to the river, scrambled into the wherry that Henry had waiting down by the archbishop's river steps and ordered the wherryman to row hard for the arches of Maidstone's fine stone bridge. Henry innocently walked back to the horses, told Piers and Banton the situation and the trio trotted out of the town gates when they opened at dawn, leading the extra mounts. We reunited with them a couple of miles along the Medway and enjoined our wherryman to stay silent or face the archbishop's wrath. John Ball would just have to wait to be freed. It would not take long.

Chapter 27

Stormbreak

For six weeks, the tax collectors had attempted to extort from the evasive, unwilling peasantry the thousands of shillings the king's nobles wanted to continue their fruitless war against the French. Often unable to extract coin from the penniless peasants, the collectors confiscated tools, animals, seed and even the commoners' very food to underscore their determination that the labouring classes must pay up. We rebels knew that the collectors were rewarded on a commission-based scale and were private citizens acting without much supervision but with orders to employ whatever tactics they thought fit to squeeze the money from people. Eventually, their harsh tactics went too far.

On the 30th day of May in the fourth year of King Richard II's reign, the storm broke. Thomas Bampton, tax commissioner for Essex, reported to John of Gaunt that the tax returns for the Hundred of Barstaple were lacking, and was ordered to ride down and investigate. 'Execute a couple of ringleaders,' Gaunt told him. 'Scare the others into paying up.'

'Bampton arrived in our village, Fobbing, with a couple of

men-at-arms and three clerks,' Adam Byrd, a waterfowler who makes his living in the local marshes, said later. Byrd was appearing before our committee in Brentford several days after Bampton's arrival to report the events he had just witnessed.

Byrd said: 'We had already been milked a year before; we expected another visit and decided we would not stand for it. We told Bampton we wouldn't pay a penny more than we already had because we were poor and the burden was unfair. Maurice Chesworth was our spokesman, and he did use some rough language: he is a cartwright and a big man who is not used to being ordered around. Bampton was arrogant and ordered Maurice to sit down and shut up but Maurice defied him, saying he was as good as any man. So, the commissioner ordered his two serjeants to arrest him.

'It was a bad mistake. We had about a hundred of us – half the village had come to show solidarity against these cruel demands – and when those soldiers laid hands on Maurice, we gave all six of them, commissioner, clerks and soldiers, a beating and stoned them out of the village. It taught them who was master. We had a bonfire and celebration that night.'

Byrd told us that, when the news reached John of Gaunt, he ordered several local jurors to present the rioters before the Chief Justice himself, Sir Robert Belknap. Three days after his officer had been beaten and expelled from Fobbing, Belknap rode to the village himself, accompanied only by three of his clerks. He formally announced his commission, said he was there to take the rioters away to gaol and demanded that the villagers pay their poll taxes. 'He was foolish to show up without any soldiers,' said Byrd, 'for we took him, his clerks and the local jurors who were his treacherous spies.' The angered Fobbing mob beat the jurors to death, bent the corpses over the village stocks and decapitated them. Then they also captured, bound and beheaded the three clerks before forcing the terrified Justice Belknap to swear on a Bible that he would never again hold such a session nor act as a justice in such inquests.

The mob released him to carry a message back to Westminster that they would not pay the poll tax and, as he scurried away, his last views of the village he had come to punish were of his royal commissions burning on a bonfire and of the heads of six of his men mounted on poles, being paraded by triumphant serfs.

On his way to London, he saw another sight: the house of John Sewale, the sheriff of Essex. It had been looted and was on fire. The sheriff was hiding in a ditch nearby, afraid for his life.

The peasantry was rising; there could be no going back and England on that May day was entering a fateful thirty days of 'inexplicable' rebellion, ruin and blood. When it ended, we labouring classes were crushed and subject to vicious punishments; it would appear to be a failure, but instead the 'failed' insurgency had laid the foundations of real freedom.

Historical Footnotes

Introduction

Bubonic plague swept across Europe between 1340 and 1353, taking its name from the blackened skin and buboes – apple-sized boils – that erupted in the groins and armpits of sufferers. The pandemic that took one-third of Europe's population in the fourteenth century was an iteration of the same pestilence that swept the Roman Empire around 542 AD and would return over and again in the sixteenth and seventeenth centuries. It has been called the world's greatest serial killer.

The Great Pestilence ravaged England during 1348 and 1349; it caused the death of about half of the population and emptied and caused the disappearance of about 1,000 villages where almost every resident died.

In Germany where many Jews had moved after being expelled from England by Edward I, accusations during the plague that Jews had poisoned wells and water supplies resulted in organised massacres of their communities that killed thousands and destroyed more than sixty large Jewish towns.

Chapter 1

Telling time was a skill in medieval England. Before clocks were invented, bells were an important way of being informed of the passage of the day. City dwellers who had the luxury of hearing nearby bells soon learned that they were rung for a range of reasons. Most common was to mark times for the clergy to pray. The church divided the 24-hour day into eight three-hour liturgical Offices or Hours, and orisons were said (in order) at Matins (midnight), Lauds (3.00 am) Prime, Terce (ninth hour), Sext (midday), Nones (3.00 pm), Vespers (after dinner) and Compline, which was about 9.00 pm or before bed.

Of course, daylight hours varied by season so the prayers which began the day would be at about 2.30 am in summer, while the midwinter start of the day was at about 6.40 am. At Christmas, a daylight 'hour' contained only forty minutes, but each night-time 'hour' was eighty minutes long. The reverse was true on St John's Day (June 24th). The inconvenient fact that daylight was not a fixed length, but many monks fasted until Nones, caused some compromises to be made and, in the twelfth century, Nones was moved to midday (hence 'noon') in England, and to mid-afternoon in France.

With the advent of mechanical clocks (Edward III introduced the earliest in his palaces in the 1350s) came a different way of regulating the day, and even if the clock was not totally accurate, everyone at least operated on the same standard.

The etiquette of eating called for the lower ranked to aid the higher and younger to help older, politely cutting meat, pulling a choice piece from the common pot or breaking bread for them. Most people shared drinking vessels; people brought their own knife to table or shared with another. Food was served on plates of wood or pewter or on hollowed-out loaves of bread – trenchers – and a **trencherman** not only ate the stew in his bread bowl but consumed the juice-soaked bowl itself.

Peasants rarely ate meat. Animals were too valuable for mere digestion and yielded milk, eggs and wool until old age made them candidates for the cooking pot. After root crops like turnips, fish was the most common food, and because no part of Britain is more than seventy miles from the coast, oysters, mussels, crab, lobster and other shell-fish could be transported live. Eels and pike were kept in vats; many castles, monasteries and manorial estates had fishponds if there was no river close by where weirs and fish traps could be employed. All that said, fish was not necessarily for the common peasant. He was not allowed to fish in ponds, rivers or lakes because the fish in them belonged to the local lord. Even if a sympathetic water bailiff let him keep a tench or two, its value was about two days' wages. Better to sell it and make do with eels, salt cod or pickled herring bought at market.

Chapter 2

Monks ate well – the fat friar was no imaginary figure – and consumed meat about 400 times a year despite Benedictine rules about never eating the flesh of quadrupeds.

The monks evaded their dietary strictures by various means, some-times interpreting 'fasting' days as merely times not to eat in the refectory, but as days when it was permissible to eat meat in the 'place of mercy' – the *misericord* – a secondary dining room originally intended for use by the ailing, who were exempted from fasting. Abuse of the system grew so rampant that a pope decreed the misericord could only be used by each brother on eighty-six days per year. The church forbade the consumption of animals for about one-third of the year, especially in Lent and Advent, and on Wednesdays, Fridays and Saturdays, all times when fish or fasting was the alternative, but devious clergy found ways around the sumptuary laws. They interpreted waterfowl, eels, puffin breasts, oysters, beavers, whale and even roast barnacle goose as falling into the category of 'fish' and escaped the strictures. Equally, the clerical consumerists interpreted the rules as exempting offal like liver, lights, tripe or kidneys, so could gorge on those meats. 'Umbles' – sheeps' entrails cooked in spiced ale – was a popular winter dish, and eggs with bacon – the latter regarded as 'collops' – was not unknown.

In even less-than-wealthy abbeys and priories, each monk was allowed a gallon of ale a day, with more for the higher clergy if they so wished, and wine was also allowed on the seventy or so saints' days. The monks also believed that the tracts of senior churchmen, like those of the nobility, were more delicate than those of commoners, so they ate many courses, starting with 'lighter' foods that 'opened the digestion' and did not bring bad humours to it.

Archery was so important to English kings of the era that every able-bodied man was by edict obliged to practise archery each week. This of course gave the monarch a fine pool of trained bowmen for his wars, a force that could shoot flat even the best-armoured knights, although often those cavalry were best defeated by the vulnerability of their horses and the thinner protection on their limbs.

War arrows were heavier than those used in hunting animals such as wolves and were ordered in thousands for medieval troops, being supplied in sheaves of two dozen. In the fourteenth century the royal garrisons obtained 51,350 sheaves, or 1,232,400 arrows, and 3,500 were retrieved from the wreck of the royal flagship Mary Rose. Most shafts were made of poplar, but ash, beech and hazel were also in use. Their length varied from 24 to 33 inches and would have been equipped with the short bodkin point, or with a small, barbed arrowhead. (No beaten-iron arrowheads survived in the wreck but military arrowheads of the day have survived elsewhere.)

Yew longbows retrieved from the wreck are computed to have had a range of up to 360 yards and required a draw weight of up to 170lbs. Modern tests of their penetration ability showed that a needle point bodkin at short range could penetrate riveted mail and even plate armour. Welsh archers used elm, a bowstave material not generally favoured by the English, who preferred yew or ash for the four-year process of drying and shaping a bowstave (and so depleted yew stocks that by 1294 yew was being imported from the continent) but the Welsh bows were noted for their astonishing stiffness and power.

Most archers protected their bow staves against water damage by coating them with a mix of tallow, wax and resin. They also hand-beat their own iron arrowheads and personally marked them. The archers were so attached to their weaponry they would often walk a battlefield, post-conflict, to retrieve their own crafted arrows.

Most vicious were the **Forest Laws,** which covered about eighty-five royal forests and chases and included in some of them as many as 700 enclosed parks to contain the animals. The only people other than himself and his nobles who were allowed to hunt in the king's chases were his woodwards and verderers. Their duties, for which they were paid two pence a day, were to exterminate the wolf, fox, badger, wildcat, pine marten, otter and even the humble squirrel to protect for the king's exclusive pleasure the hart, hind, hare and wild boar that shared the territory.

A freeman – not a peasant – had the right to kill a deer on his own land but was not permitted to follow it into a royal forest. In a case where a franklin built a buckstall – a long net used to snare deer – two bowshots from a royal preserve, he was heavily fined. When he boldly did it again, he escaped the old Norman punishment of having his eyes put out but was condemned to worse: he was publicly hanged after the hart's antlers were nailed to his head.

Chapter 5

The network of English roads built by the Romans has done considerable service over the centuries and they still form a backbone for transport today. Tom Thatcher travelled on Watling Street to reach Dover (the word 'street' comes from the Latin *strata* meaning paved) but he may well also have used the great north roads of Ermine Street, Dere Street or the very ancient Fosse Way in his travels. It is possible even today to walk on surfaces set down two millennia ago: the Roman Watling Street is so named (Wattelingstrete) in a charter of 1285 and a stretch of it in Red Scar, east of Preston, Lancashire, was exposed in 1977 and remains accessible. Appropriately named Roman Way, it is sited by Longridge Road, Preston, in an industrial estate just east of the M6 motorway. Look near a landscaped pond that was once a watering hole for Samian cavalry riding to the Roman camp of Ribchester should you wish to walk where the legions once did. It lies just off Roman Way; the old road is behind the hedge. Its informative display board has sadly disappeared. Not far away, the old road is remembered in the modern Watling Street Road, Fulwood.

Chapter 9

Arrow extraction: King Henry V, at that time sixteen-year-old Prince Hal, took an arrow to the face at the battle of Shrewsbury in 1403. It penetrated under his right eye and beside his nose and went five or six inches into his head, narrowly missing arteries and the brain stem. A number of barber-surgeons attempted to remove the barbed missile with techniques that varied from using hot wax to ease it from the wound to trying to make it come out by prayer. None of the efforts of what the prince called the *lewd chattering leeches* worked.

John Bradmore, surgeon and metalworker, arrived at Kenilworth Castle to do what he could, and performed a remarkable feat of battlefield medicine. He chose a traditional technique, using elder pith probes of increasing size to match the width and depth of the wound, into which he poured sterilising honey and opened access to the arrowhead. He devised and made a special corkscrew-like tool whose slender screw-threaded tongs went into the socket of the arrowhead, were expanded to grip it and so allowed it to be pulled free. The prince's life was saved.

The surgeon continued intensive treatment for three weeks, making the probes increasingly smaller and cleaning the wound with wine so it healed naturally and gradually closed. Bradmore, who had once been imprisoned for counterfeiting coins, was rewarded with a royal pension of ten marks a year, an amount sufficient to buy six draught horses or to build a modest hall and chamber. He was also appointed to the lucrative post of Searcher of the Port of London and became a regular medical attendant at court.

Setting injured/broken ribs was another matter. Physicians opted for the oldest method of holding a fracture: the use of wooden splints.

The Egyptians used bark wrapped in linen, or stiffened bandages like those used for embalming. Hippocrates wrote of using wooden splints and recommended exercise to prevent muscle atrophy. The ancient Greeks also used bandages stiffened with waxes and resins while the Roman Celsus, writing in 30 CE, describes the use of splints and starch-stiffened bandages. The medieval Italian bonesetters of Salerno had a technique of using a flour, egg and lime mix which set.

Chapter 14

The Battle of Crecy (Saturday 26 August 1346)

The tidal ford at **Blanchetaque,** long gone since the Somme was canalised, was a limestone ridge that ran across the river, making a causeway in the riverbed, hence the name 'white platform'.

Prime: the clergy's Offices of prayer were not evenly spaced but took account of shorter winter days so that the canonical bells that would sound for Matins at 6.40 am in midwinter would chime at 2.30 am in midsummer, and at 5.00 am at equinox. In August 1346, Prime, the second Office of the day, would have been marked around 4.00 am, as daylight was dawning. The battle for the ford at Blanchetaque was fought about five hours later.

The Genoese, King Philip's only professional soldiers, were indeed tired. Jean Froissart said they had marched six leagues (eighteen miles) that day, in full armour and carrying their heavy crossbows. *'They told the Constable they were not in a condition to do any great thing in battle,'* the chronicler wrote, but the Earl of Alencon dismissed them as 'scoundrels' when they retreated from the English arrows. King Philip's forces lacked strong leadership since the Constable of France, Raoul of Brienne had been captured at Caen.

The battle took the lives of the elite of the French nobility, about 1,500 knights, and as many as 16,000 common soldiers, a considerable number of whom were crushed to death by their comrades' undisciplined advance. The English, who lost about 300 dead, withstood fifteen or so French cavalry charges. King Philip himself was wounded in the face by an arrow strike and the gallant, blind King John of Bohemia died when he was led into the melée with his horse tethered to that of two of his knights' mounts. His request was to be led into the engagement *'that I may strike one stroke with my sword'*. His body was found in front of the Black Prince's line, the horses still tied together.

The chronicler **Jean Froissart** says that Lords Cobham and Stafford, with three heralds to interpret the arms and two secretaries to record the names, came across eighty banners on the battlefield and counted the bodies of eleven princes, 1,200 knights and about 30,000 common soldiers, a number he likely exaggerated.

Chapter 18

Chevauchée: When the Black Prince prepared for his **great raids**, he followed the precepts of Charlemagne, issuing instructions to his horsemen on what they should take with them: shield, lance, sword, dagger, bow and arrows. In the carts: axes, planes, augers, boards, spades, iron shovels, plus a supply of food, clothing and arms. (Medieval soldiers supplied their own food as best they could.) Prince Edward did more: he established advance supply dumps to reduce the equipment he must carry, kept carts to a minimum, used a vast horse herd of riding and sumpters, hauled no siege engines and took only minimal bridging equipment. He was not interested in investing well-fortified towns or castles: his intent was to travel fast, to create havoc and wreck confidence in the French king's ability to protect his subjects.

Chapter 19

Coronation Stone: **The Stone of Scone** (the Scottish town pronounced 'Scoon') is a block of red sandstone used for centuries as the coronation seat of Scottish kings. After Edward I's appropriation of it, the stone became part of the chair on which England's monarchs were crowned. (Queen Elizabeth II was the last, in 1953.)

Sometimes called 'Jacob's Pillow' or the 'Stone of Destiny', it was originally kept at Scone Abbey and is of Old Red Sandstone quarried nearby. Students stole the stone from Westminster in 1950, but it was recovered five months later. It was returned to Scotland in 1996, with a provision to use it for future English coronations. Some claim that the real Stone of Destiny was a large meteorite found on Dunsinane Hill and that the canny monks of Scone fooled Edward with a fake.

Chapter 22

Medieval medicine: Physicians of the day were great believers in herbal remedies. Alexander Neckham (1157–1217 CE), Bishop of Cirencester, was a scholar and theologian with a keen interest in medical science who grew a not-atypical garden of medicinal herbs including saffron, thyme, borage, ragwort, valerian and myrtle. Traces of these crushed herbs were found in a thirteenth century Chester cesspit and, as they were not normally regarded as edible, the find indicates their use in medicine. Most prominent was corncockle (*Agrostemma*) which was commonly used in the Middle Ages as a laxative.

Chapter 23

The falconer, called an 'austringer' if he trained the white-chested goshawk ('goosehawk') often had silver chain jesses made for his peregrine and kept her on a perch in his bedchamber as well as sometimes taking her with him, hooded and jessed, on his wrist as he walked about. It was all part of acclimatising the bird to his presence and to everyday sights and surroundings.

Some hawkers liked to be accompanied by their ladies on their outings to the field, for women found their smaller hands an advantage in managing the straps, thongs and rings which held the raptors; other men complained the women's presence turned hawking into a frivolous and effeminate pastime. The sport also yielded some modern terms: the cadger or cadge-boy who carried the perching frame for the hooded ('hoodwinked') falcons had little to do once the birds were released to fly, so loafed about with the empty frame on his back hoping for tips, hence the term 'cadging'. A 'cast' was a pair of hawks, a 'lese' was a trio of birds. The birds were 'mewed up' in a mews, which was a place where they were kept while moulting, or 'casting' their feathers. In time, many mews were converted to stables and eventually to fashionable town housing.

The clergy were technically forbidden to hawk or hunt but did so with impunity, and so valued their pastime that the Bishop of Ely once excommunicated those who stole his personal hawk from her perch in the choir during divine service. Even unborn falcons were protected: anyone convicted of taking or damaging hawks' eggs was to be jailed for a year and a day, and also must pay a heavy fine, half of which went to the king, half to the landowner on whose property the eggs were found.

Chapter 24

Joan Plantagenet, the Fair Maid of Kent, was the daughter of the Earl of Kent and granddaughter of King Edward I and was noted not just for her beauty, but also for a controversial marital history. The court historian Jean Froissart described her 'the most beautiful lady in England – and the most amorous.'

At age twelve, Joan secretly married her father's steward, the twenty-eight-year-old knight Thomas Holland, just before he left for war. In his absence, her mother pushed Joan into a lucrative marriage to William Montacute, heir to the Earl of Salisbury, a close friend of King Edward III. Montacute grew up with the king's son, Edward of Woodstock, later known as the Black Prince.

When Holland returned and found that his wife had been married to someone else, he successfully petitioned the Pope to have the union annulled. The couple reunited and had four children before Thomas died, when Montacute's boyhood friend Edward the Black Prince entered the picture. At a time when royals married for political or diplomatic reasons, Joan was an unlikely bride for a future king of England. She was a widow with four children; she was Edward's cousin; there was no political advantage to be gained by the marriage, nor would it enhance the prestige of the English throne.

Worse, Joan's history could be problematic for the succession to the throne, as the Black Prince's heirs might be judged ineligible. King Edward recognised this and petitioned Pope Innocent VI for a dispensation to confirm the legitimacy of any royal heir. At first, the request was denied. Edward then claimed the prince had recently secretly married Joan. Rather than offend the king, the Pope acceded to the request and declared the legitimacy of any future offspring. Joan, coronated as the first Princess of Wales, was a model wife who gave Edward two boys and lived to see her ten-year-old son crowned King Richard II.

Sceptics of her 'secret marriage' to Thomas Holland slyly called her 'The Virgin of Kent', alluding to her more common label: 'Fair Maid of Kent'.

Chapter 26

Sword step: spiral staircases were built with a clockwise rotation so a right-handed defender could more easily stab downwards at an attacker, who conversely would be fighting more awkwardly back-handed (if he were right-handed) and uphill around the central pillar. Many steps in strategic buildings incorporated a single step two or three inches higher than the others, to cause an unwary attacker to stumble and put himself at the mercy of the defender.

Historical Characters

King Edward III (Edward of Windsor) 1312–1377. Crowned king at age fourteen, Edward three years later led a coup against his controlling regents and regained his throne to begin a long and successful reign which saw the evolution of parliament and significant English military gains in France and Scotland. An excellent general who made his nation into a formidable military power, he was enamoured of Arthurian principles of chivalry which he did not always follow. Generally regarded as a popular and merciful monarch, he founded the Order of the Garter.

Queen Isabella (the 'She-Wolf of France') 1295–1358. Daughter of Philip IV of France, she was married at age twelve to Edward II. Largely ignored by her husband during his infatuation with Piers Gaveston, Isabella took her son the prince to France, raised an army, deposed her husband and put Edward of Windsor on the throne. In time, the young king seized control from his regents, executed his mother's lover and banished Isabella to remote Castle Rising, Norfolk.

Queen Philippa (Philippa of Hainault) 1315–1369. Philippa was only twelve years old when she was betrothed to Edward of Windsor as a pawn to gain support for Queen Isabella's invasion of England, but the marriage was a success and Edward remained devoted to his wife.

Edward, Prince of Wales (Black Prince, Edward of Woodstock) 1330–1376. Raised by his father Edward III as a warrior, sixteen-year-old Edward led the vanguard of the English army to a defining victory at Crecy after ravaging northern France. Edward assumed the insignia of three ostrich feathers and his 'Ich Dien' motto (I serve) from the arms of the slain King John of Bohemia. He later stained his reputation by ordering civilian massacres. That, and his black armour, earned him his nickname. Edward pre-deceased his father, so never ascended to the English throne.

John of Gaunt (Duke of Lancaster) 1340–1399. Younger brother of the Black Prince and father of King Henry IV, founder of the royal House of Lancaster. John, who was born in Ghent, was unpopular for the brutal taxations levied to cover the costs of his struggling military campaigns and acted as an imperious regent for his young nephew. He was also regarded with suspicion for his actions in taking financial advantage of his ailing father, the king.

Joan Plantagenet (the Fair Maid of Kent) 1328–1385. Joan, whose childhood guardian was Queen Philippa, claimed a prior, secret wedding at age twelve to the Lancashire knight Sir Thomas Holland and gained a papal annulment of her marriage to William Montacute, Earl of Salisbury. On Holland's death, she married her cousin the Black Prince and became the first Princess of Wales. Their son became King Richard II at age ten.

King Richard II 1367–1400. The boy king who met the rebellious peasants was later pronounced an unfit monarch by Parliament but resisted efforts to unseat him and became a brutal tyrant who broke all the promises he made to pacify the peasant rebels.

Sir Robert Knollys (Cheshire knight, infamous freebooter) 1325–1407. One of the Black Prince's most important captains, he scorched the continent during the Hundred Years' War and helped suppress the Peasants' Uprising.

John Wycliffe (priest, theologian, scholar, reformer). 1325–1384. He taught that Christianity could be improved by better knowledge of the scriptures, questioned the church on transubstantiation, veneration of saints and the legitimacy of papacy.

John Ball (priest, Lollard leader) 1338–1381. Forerunner of Wycliffe, radical and firebrand preacher who taught the equality of men.

Wat Tyler (social reformer, peasant leader) 1341–1381. Opposed the poll taxes and led a mob from Canterbury to London, where he was killed.

John Wrawe (former chaplain, vicar of Ringsfield) c. 1340–1382. Led peasants into Suffolk, sacked the abbey at Bury St Edmunds, was captured and executed.

Richard Whittington (royal financier, alderman, sheriff, Mayor of London) c. 1350s–1423. A son with no inheritance, he left Gloucester for London, became a mercer with high profile clients including King Richard II and was elevated after making loans to the king.

Jack Straw (Rakestrawe) c. 1340–1381. Rebel leader noted for his fiery speeches from atop a haywain.

Acknowledgements

No author writes alone, however much he protests that he does. Inspiration and direction came to me from Lume Books' publishing team, who midwifed more than a dozen of my historical fiction works to delivery. For all that they do, my grateful thanks.

Much gratitude, too, to my patient wife Jennie who suffers conversation about matters medieval for months on end; to my daughters Claire and Rachel for their legal and publishing insights, and for creating my fine website; to the admirable Kelvin Jones for his cartography and to the King's College, London, Fine Rolls Project team; to chroniclers like the monks of St Mary's Abbey, York, who wrote the Anonimalle Chronicle of 1333–1381, and the chivalric poet-historian Jean Froissart, all of whose work has so aided my research. Many of the medieval annalists long ago became dust, but their view of events is both relevant and vibrant today. I am also grateful to the more recent transcriptionists and historians Andre Réville (1896), Charles Oman (1906) and Keith Feiling (1950) for their diligent insights and illumination.

Englishman Paul Bannister spent his journalism career on national newspapers and the BBC in Britain and the USA and now makes his home in the Pacific Northwest of the United States. He has two six-book series published by Lume Books, London: the 'Lost Emperor' volumes which begin with 'Arthur Britannicus,' and the 'Crusader' series. All are available on Amazon, as soon will be his autobiographical 'Press Gang' (Fall, 2022) and 'Tabloid Man & the Baffling Chair of Death' (2013). More details: **www.bannisterbooks.com**

Oregon, July 2022.

CPSIA information can be obtained
at www.ICGtesting.com
Printed in the USA
BVHW032331060223
658028BV00012B/465

9 781839 015175